Budgie, Bridge
and Big Djinn

First published in India in 2019 by HarperCollins Children's Books
An imprint of HarperCollins *Publishers*
A-75, Sector 57, Noida, Uttar Pradesh 201301, India
www.harpercollins.co.in

2 4 6 8 10 9 7 5 3 1

Text © Ranjit Lal 2019

P-ISBN: 978-93-5357-321-8
E-ISBN: 978-93-5357-437-6

Ranjit Lal asserts the moral right
to be identified as the author of this work.

Typeset in 11/15.5 Bembo Std at
Manipal Digital Systems, Manipal

Printed and bound at
Thomson Press (India) Ltd

MIX
Paper
FSC FSC® C010615

Budgie, Bridge and Big Djinn

Ranjit Lal

HarperCollins*Children'sBooks*

1

Fourteen-year-old Shoma looked around the breakfast table that morning and shuddered. She wished so much she could take her breakfast out into the verandah and have it with Big Djinn, but she knew that it would upset Nani. As usual, Nani sat at the head of the table, making sure that everyone was being well fed. She ran a five-room Home-stay called Mehegtal Cloud-house, 7000 feet up in the mountains, a three-hour drive from Nainital.

At the moment, it was the guests that were causing Shoma distress. Specifically, her obnoxious cousins, Siddharth and Aditi, and their parents, Sohan Uncle and Vinita Aunty, who still hadn't turned up for breakfast. They were here from London to take part in a major International Birdwatcher's Seminar that was to be held at Mehegtal Resorts nearby in a week's time.

This morning at the breakfast table, there was also the strange, silent teenaged boy, Brijesh, the fifteen to sixteen-year-old whom Nani had fetched all the way from Mumbai just last night. Two evenings ago, Nani had received a telephone call, and Shoma had never seen her grandmother get so agitated before.

'Okay, dear,' she had told whoever she had been speaking to, 'you just hang in there, darling – I'm coming to get you. You have to get out of there as soon as possible!' She had hastily packed an overnighter and left late that evening.

'I have to go to Mumbai, sweetie,' she told Shoma, 'it's a bit of an emergency! I'll be in touch.' Then she had instructed Annie, Cloud-house's manageress, to make up a bedroom.

'You're bringing someone back with you, Nani?' Shoma asked.

'Yes, dear, he's the only son of one of my most brilliant and lovely pupils who sadly passed away recently.'

'Oh, what happened to your student?' Shoma asked.

'She had cancer, dear.'

'Oh – and doesn't the boy have a papa?'

Nani's eyes got flinty. 'Of course he does, but he's the problem. He's an abusive alcoholic, very violent and in no state to look after Brijesh. So, I'm going to bring Brijesh here for a month or so and we'll see how things go.'

Nani had taught in a school in Mumbai where Nana had worked for many years before Nana had died. After that she had retired and moved to Mehegtal, back into her own papa's rambling old house, where she opened the Home-stay.

Nani had arrived last night accompanied by the boy, who looked pale and tired and sported what looked suspiciously like a black eye and a livid contusion on his cheek. He was pulling along one small suitcase and one large, flat wooden box and carried a bulging backpack.

Shoma couldn't imagine what it would be like to not have a mother. Not that she saw her own parents very often. They had separated five years ago and were still fighting tooth and nail over everything they had possessed – including her, she thought, which is why they had dumped her on Nani for 'the time being', which had lasted five years already! They thought it was better that Shoma didn't witness their bitter acrimony first-hand. Of course, they loved her very much – or so they kept saying. They certainly showered her with lavish gifts every time they met her. Her mom had given her fancy, designer outfits and even a snazzy imported make-up kit; and her dad a fabulous mountain bike and, of all things, a small green fiberglass boat with an actual engine, which Shoma had delightedly christened *Rubadubdub*. It was a pretty irresponsible gift, Nani thought, considering that Shoma couldn't swim very well. Nani had insisted that she wore her life jacket and informed everyone at home when she went out boating on Mehegtal Lake. But then, Shoma's dad, Dalbir, had never been a very responsible sort, and Ramona, Shoma's mom, had been one of those fashionable types who spent her time in airy-fairy gossip with high society ladies.

Nani had had to hide her tears when she had first spotted nine-year-old Shoma at Kathgodam railway station five years ago, timorously holding the hand of her maid, Annie, and looking around with big dark eyes. Her curly, wonderfully frizzy hair had been tied up in a high ponytail and her little snub nose and cheeks were already pink with the cold. She was huddled up in a brand new beige windcheater and faded blue jeans. 'You looked like a lost little budgerigar,' Nani had said, and the name stuck.

'Nani, you like picking up abandoned waifs!' Shoma had teased her mischievously when she had gone to say goodnight after Nani had settled Brijesh into his room and retired to her own. 'First you picked me up, then you found Djinn and now this fellow!' And actually, the place had suited Annie perfectly too – she was now manageress of the Home-stay, organizing meals and ensuring the guests were well looked after and taking care of all the house-keeping. Kusum, Nani's old help—again someone she had rescued from a violent husband—now did the cooking and looked after Shoma.

Shoma thought Big Djinn had been the best thing that Nani could have picked up. Just a day or two after Shoma had arrived at Cloud-house, Nani had spotted him staggering about miserably in the rain just outside Mehegtal town – a fat, bedraggled black and gold puppy, maybe six weeks old, very furry and with pleading honey-coloured eyes, massive lion paws and a curly, bushy tail. She'd brought him home and Shoma had immediately forgotten her homesickness and fallen all over the little fellow. The pup too had seemed to have sensed a kindred soul and had followed her around everywhere ever since. It was only when the pup had been taken to the vet, Dr. Rathore, for a checkup that Nani wondered if this time she had bitten off more than she could chew. As Shoma watched wide-eyed, the vet had examined the pup, raised an eyebrow and turned to Nani.

'Umm, ma'am, what we seem to have here is a cross between a Tibetan mastiff and a German shepherd. He's going to be a handful! He's going to be a very big, strong, stubborn dog! Are you sure you'll be able to keep him?'

'Oh,' Nani said, nonplussed. But when she saw Shoma gazing lovingly at the squirming little fellow, she told the vet, 'Well, he seems to have taken to the little girl, so I think we will.'

'Very well! But you should know: these are outdoor dogs, very good guards, strong-willed and very faithful to their family. They're aloof with outsiders … Are you still sure you want to keep him?'

'Oh,' Nani frowned. When you ran a homestay, you had outsiders all the time! But she was a resolute lady too, not one to give up easily.

'We'll keep him. He'll be good for Budgie!'

'Nani, I'm going to call him Djinn!' Shoma said excitedly on the way back from the vet's. 'He moves so quietly, just like one. And I'm going to train him well!'

Nani had watched with surprised delight as the little girl had gone about 'training' the dog, which very soon was much bigger and stronger than her. So much so that now Shoma called him Big Djinn! She barked out her commands, 'sit, stay, come, heel!' firmly and clearly, meaning what she was saying – and Djinn soon realized this. And he listened! Shoma could be a bossy little thing when she put her mind to it. But she brushed him and took him out for runs when she went biking and had even taken him out in *Rubadubdub*. Once Big Djinn had accepted that she was the boss, it was easy. But he lived up to his reputation too. He was protective of her almost to a fault, following her around everywhere, even to school. The vet had been right too – he was very much an outdoors dog. In spring and summer, he slept outside in the verandah, and during the monsoons and winter just inside the big drawing room doors that opened out into the verandah. He didn't like coming indoors very much, which suited Nani because he didn't get in the way of her guests. He was a gorgeous, if wolfish, sort of fellow: massively built, his coat was thick and silky, coal black with gold highlights; his eyes brown, almond-shaped and wise. He was calm and aloof and only got a bit goofy when Shoma rubbed his massive chest and tickled his ears and baby-talked nonsense to him.

He had caused a great deal of turmoil the first time he had followed her to school. Shoma was usually picked up by the school van near Cloud-house's car park and donkey stables, which was a 30-minute steep up-and-down trek from the house itself, along a narrow forest trail across a high mountain ridge. The Home-stay did have a party of seven sturdy donkeys to ferry visitors and their luggage to and fro. Shoma had christened them Dumpy, Grumpy, Stumpy, Dopey, Frumpy, Clumpy and Snoozy, inspired by the names of the seven dwarfs. However, the relatively difficult access put off all but the keenest visitors, which suited Nani just fine.

'I don't want any riff-raff rowdies coming here!' Nani had made clear.

'Nani, Big Djinn won't let them come here, so don't worry!' Shoma had told her.

But that day, Big Djinn had jumped clear over the garden gate and followed Shoma all the way to her school. Shoma's school, 'Mehegtal Gramin Paathshala', was a single-storey building painted pale yellow with a red tin roof, with just 10 classrooms and maybe 100 pupils. It was located about three kilometres outside Mehegtal town proper, adjoining a dark and whispery pine, oak and deodar forest. It was very much a 'do-it-yourself' school where class monitors were entrusted to open and clean the classrooms every morning before their teachers rolled up and had to ring the school bell and sometimes even hold assembly. (Of course, they assigned other students to do all the actual hard work!). But it was an excellent school and produced most of the state's toppers in the CBSE exams every year.

That morning when Mrs. Sethi, the principal, turned up at around 10 a.m., she was brought up short by this enormous furry black dog quietly lying outside Shoma's classroom. For a moment, she had thought he was a baby bear. Other teachers who had seen him had given him a wide berth in the corridor when they passed by, and he had just ignored them. The watchman too had just let him pass when he trotted quietly through the gates. Big Djinn had that sort of effect on people – they didn't want to mess with him in any way.

'Djinn, what are you doing here?' Shoma had exclaimed, 'you followed me!' The dog acknowledged this with a brief wag of his tail.

Shoma's friends kept their distance too.

'My God, he looks like a cross between a bear and a wolf!' one of them said, in awe.

'He won't do anything!' Shoma had assured them. 'He's just checking on me. Really, Djinn, you should go home now!'

But that was one thing Big Djinn was not about to do. On his way here through the forest, and quite near the school, he had caught scent of that implacable dog enemy – the leopard. Shoma, alas, was summoned to the principal's office later that morning.

'Shoma, you'll have to keep your dog at home. We can't have that monstrous animal sitting in the corridor. He might attack the children. As it is they're so frightened of him, as are most of us!'

'Ma'am, he won't do anything. He likes keeping to himself.'

'I'm sorry, dear, but he can't come here. I don't want to see him here tomorrow. Is that clear?'

But by the afternoon, Mrs. Sethi and everyone else in the school had changed their minds! During the lunch break the children had, as usual, spilled out into the large grassy playground that abutted the forest. Some ran around madly, others sat under the great pine trees and ate their lunch. The teachers were sitting at the tables near the flower beds, from where they could keep an eye on the children, eat their lunch and enjoy the sunshine. Shoma had settled down for lunch under one of the massive pine trees, sharing her kathi rolls with Djinn, one arm around the big dog's shaggy neck. Suddenly, a panic-stricken scream rent the air. Djinn pricked up his ears and turned his head towards the direction of the shriek – as did everyone else in the playground.

Reena Didi, the Head Girl, had just come out of the girls' washroom, which was located in a separate little building, right next to the great brooding forest. And the leopard that Djinn had smelt earlier that morning had just stepped out of the forest, his golden eyes glinting hungrily as he belly-crawled towards the girl. He had watched her go in and had waited for her. A quick leap, a vicious neck bite and he would drag his victim back into the forest, up a tree and eat it in peace. Backed up against the washroom wall, Reena looked at him in terror as he drew back his lips and snarled. Then she crumpled to the ground in a dead faint. She had just made things easier for the leopard.

'Djinn, *no!*' Shoma shrieked as the huge dog hurtled full tilt towards the hateful enemy with a deep-throated bark and growl. The leopard had just turned his head to check this new threat when Djinn leapt at him, fastening his teeth around the leopard's neck, growling ferociously and trying to pin him down. Djinn wore a spiked steel anti-leopard collar which protected his neck, but the leopard was no pushover. Flat on his back now, with Djinn at his throat, he frantically lashed out with his claws, his golden eyes blazing. But Djinn would not let go. Somehow the leopard wriggled free and fled like a skimming stone back into the forest. Djinn gave a deep-throated bark of contempt as he watched him go and then trotted back to Shoma, cool as you please, his tail curled around his back, wagging stiffly.

'Baby, are you all right?' Shoma exclaimed, running her hands through his thick coat. She nearly fainted when she saw her hands come out covered in blood! 'Oh my God, he's raked you with his claws!'

But Djinn had also certainly saved Reena's life. Still trembling, the tall girl was now shakily picking herself up as the teachers and Mrs. Sethi rushed towards her. They had seen everything. Shoma ran up to them, Djinn trotting resolutely beside her.

'Ma'am, he's hurt. Can I take him to the vet?' she pleaded.

'Oh my God, the poor fellow!' After assuring herself that Reena was fine, Mrs. Sethi organized the school's van to take Shoma and Djinn to Dr. Rathore's clinic in Mehegtal town, accompanied by her class teacher.

Djinn stood stoically on the vet's examining table as the two deep gouges on either side of his ribs were cleaned and stitched up as Shoma looked on anxiously.

'He's a strong, calm fellow!' Dr. Rathore said admiringly, giving the dog an antibiotic injection. 'He'll be just fine! Bring him over in a week's time and I'll remove the stitches.' He smiled. 'But try and keep him away from leopards!'

Back at school later that afternoon, Shoma had been summoned to Mrs. Sethi's office once again. Djinn waited patiently outside.

'Dear, after what happened this afternoon, I think you can bring your dog to school every day if you like,' she said. 'He saved Reena's life!'

'Thank you, ma'am!'

Since then, Shoma and Big Djinn would go to school together in the van every day – and Djinn even permitted some of Shoma's friends to stroke and pet him. If these children were a part of Shoma's pack, then he thought it was his duty to protect them too. In a way, he had become the school's mascot. The arrangement had suited Nani well too, because now she didn't have to worry about her guests being frightened by 'that huge bear of a dog' prowling around. At school, Djinn would settle down outside Shoma's classroom, patiently on guard against rogue leopards and generally ignoring the teachers and other kids.

★★★★★

'You know, I had a pair of red-billed leiothrixes, down by the lake!' fifteen-year-old Siddharth announced importantly at the breakfast table. Shoma rolled her eyes.

'You mean you ate them?' she asked sweetly. 'Ew! I nearly threw up just now!'

Siddharth, with his smooth peach cheeks and slicked-back hair, shook his head disparagingly.

'Don't be stupid, where did you get such an idea?'

'Well, you said you "had them". How? Tandoori? Fried? Or raw?'

'Ha-ha! When I said I "had them", I meant I saw them,' he explained unctuously. God, but was she thick! So ... so provincial! Well, she went to a local school outside a one-street hick town, so what else could you expect?

'Well, why don't you say what you mean then? When you said you "had" them it means you either ate them or have them as pets ... And besides, anyone can see them!'

'Like you, I suppose,' Siddharth's sister, Aditi, said sarcastically. 'You live here and haven't seen anything. All you do is ride your stupid bike all day, with your stupid dog running beside you from morning to evening.'

'Well, when *I* say I "had" a fish it means I caught it in the lake and fried it and ate it,' Shoma said carefully, mimicking Siddharth's voice perfectly. 'And Djinn is not a stupid dog!'

Aditi was one of those girls who Shoma felt needed a tight smack every time she opened her prissy pink mouth. So did Siddharth. Just because they went to school in England, they spoke in posh, high-pitched falsetto accents which really got her goat, and behaved as if everyone else was hugely uncivilized compared to them. Why couldn't they talk like normal people instead of affecting such airs?

She tossed her ponytail angrily.

'You don't know the half of what I might and might not have seen! You come here for a month every year, so what do you know?'

Thank God they were only here for a month! And it really was amazing some of the things Shoma had seen and noticed and painted in the five years she had been here. The way, if you half-closed your eyes, the beautiful wildflowers in the meadow going down to the lake's edge, rocked and swayed in the breeze, their colours blurring and shimmering into each other. The way iridescent little beetles could look like jewels and precious stones, changing colours depending on the angle of the light. The way Mehegtal could turn into a platter of pure dazzling gold at dawn and dusk. And shimmer silver at midday like a sheet of mercury – and before and after that, a deep sapphire blue or emerald green, depending on the season and the angle of the light.

'Look, Djinn,' Shoma had said to the dog early one morning, 'we have all the gold in the world right at our feet!'

Nani's large rambling stone and ivy-covered Home-stay was perched on a mountain ledge, on the southern bank of Mehegtal Lake. The spacious drawing and dining rooms, with their huge fireplaces and floor-to-ceiling windows, were on the ground floor and opened out into a deep verandah which overlooked a sloping garden, a lovely flower meadow and the lake itself. The bedrooms were on the first floor, all with huge picture windows that overlooked the same breathtaking view. The house was surrounded by steeply forested mountain slopes, and beyond the lake's northern shore, you could see waterfalls gushing down the slopes. And way above and beyond, the high Himalayas, glittering with ice and snow, stretched right across the horizon.

Mehegtal Lake itself was about 2.5 kilometres long from east to west, and 1.5 kilometres at its widest point from south to north. It was shaped like an 'L' with three small but thickly forested islands forming a 'U' towards its western shore and one smaller one off its northern shore. The lake was surrounded by steep mountain slopes, with a narrow pathway clinging to its shoreline, interspersed by streams and waterfalls tumbling down the slopes. Shoma hugely enjoyed biking around the lake, particularly pushing her bike up some of the narrow paths leading up the mountains and then freewheeling down madly with Djinn racing delightedly beside her. On several occasions, she had landed straight into the lake with a humongous splash!

★★★★★

Mehegtal was rather inaccessible because the mountains here were steep and rocky and remote and there were no proper roads, which had kept developers at bay for a long time.

This was why, some three years ago, Shoma had been slightly disquieted when she spotted men with what looked like telescopes wandering around the north-west corner of the mountain ridges rising above the lake. They kept peering into their instruments and making notes.

'There must be a road leading up there we don't know about,' she had told Djinn, watching them through binoculars with a sense of vague unease. She was right to be uneasy. A month later, when she heard the distinct 'thwack' of axes biting into wood and the sound of heavy engines and machinery and chainsaws, she had rushed to Nani.

'Nani, they're cutting down the forest on the side of the mountains there!'

Nani had sighed.

'Yes, dear, I know,' she had shrugged. 'A very rich developer wants to build a resort there and a golf course right on top. They're going to shore up the bare mountainside with soil and rocks and probably cement, till it's level with the top, to make a kind of tableland on which they'll plant their golf course. We're going to have a rather disturbed time while they're on the job!'

'But … but …!' Shoma had been appalled.

'It's a project by one of the country's richest builders and property developers, Suraj Mukhi Enterprises,' Nani had said. 'In fact, Mr. Suraj Mukhi is an old friend of Sohan Uncle's from school. I wouldn't be surprised if Sohan Uncle told him about this place!'

'But … but is he allowed to … to do all this, cut the trees and all?' Shoma had sputtered indignantly. Nani had sighed sadly again.

'Mr. Suraj Mukhi is a very, very wealthy and powerful person. Some say he has more money and influence than even the Dabanis. So, he usually gets what he wants. He knows a lot of important political people very well, including the Prime Minister; it's said he secretly pays for their election campaigns. He's got all the permissions and clearances required from the government. The government thinks it'll be good for the economy – more tourists will turn up and the area will be developed,' she had shrugged. 'I suppose they'll be very rich golfing types wanting to have weddings and parties here …'

The project had got underway with feverish speed. Thousands of magnificent old pine, fir, oak and deodar trees were felled from the slopes and the top of the mountain. An endless convoy of giant trucks had groaned up the mountain, loaded with soil and boulders, and an army of labourers began to work, gradually levelling the slope till the ridge top. Massive JCBs and bulldozers had somehow roared up and flattened the mountaintop into a smooth if slightly slanting tableland, which was then drenched with fertilizer and pesticides and herbicides and planted over with sterile golf-course grass.

It was a truly gargantuan project, because the golf course was at least 1.5 kilometres long all along what was once a mountain ridge, so the amount of soil and boulders needed was huge (and stolen, it was said, from nearby river-beds). A helipad had been built on a flattened section and blue and white helicopters would often clatter their way over the mountains, presumably with big bosses on board. The golf clubhouse was built at one end of the course and the resort rooms, along with a villa for Mr. Suraj Mukhi and his family, were on a long narrow rocky ledge some way below the tableland. Painted a sickly pea-green and mustard-yellow, the resort and villa sat like toads' warts on the mountain ledge, their huge, one-way plate glass windows flashing blindly in the sun. Thankfully, it was almost impossible for anyone to access Cloud-house from the resort on foot because the terrain was just impossible, riven with deep ravines and waterfalls and treacherous cliff faces. But you could, of course, more easily access it by helicopter or boat. One afternoon, Shoma had returned home from school, ambling happily along on Grumpy with Djinn at her side. As she dismounted and approached the front door, the dog had stiffened, the hair on his neck rising. A deep malevolent growl rumbled low down in his throat.

'What is it, Djinn?' Shoma held him by the collar and looked around. It could be another leopard.

'Nani!' she called, 'I'm home!'

She found Nani sitting in the drawing room with company. There were three men in the room, one sitting on the settee alongside her and two in the armchairs around the coffee table. The man sitting next to her was in an immaculate raw-silk kurta and tight churidar and sported a bright red tilak. He had a huge pakora nose, fish-like lips and watery peering eyes that shifted around all the time. He wore huge gold rings studded with stones on nearly every caterpillar-like finger and a magnum-sized gold watch. His hair was slick and black. The other two men were in suits and also had oily slicked-back hair.

Nani smiled at her. 'Hello, dear! How was school? Say namaste, dear. This is Shri Suraj Mukhiji – he's just come to say hello. Mukhiji, this is my granddaughter Shoma.'

Djinn rumbled like an incipient volcano and Shoma didn't dare let go of him. She inclined her head prettily.

'Namaste uncle,' she said, 'I'll just take Djinn to the verandah …'

Out in the verandah she saw the blue and white helicopter standing in the middle of the flower meadow, with its pilot lounging about outside.

'It's okay, Djinn. They're guests, well, sort of,' she told the rumbling dog, 'Take it easy, boy!'

Kusum brought her tea out into the verandah and about fifteen minutes later she had to hold on to Djinn yet again, as the three men emerged with Nani and made their way down the stone steps towards the helicopter. It made a huge noise as it took off, flattening the flowers in the field with its wash. Djinn continued to growl steadily as they watched it go.

'Nani, Djinn didn't like them *at all!*' Shoma declared. 'What did they want?'

'Oh, it was just a courtesy call; the resort will be opening shortly and they invited me to the inauguration and asked if I could put up some of their guests.'

What Nani omitted to mention was that Mr. Suraj Mukhi had made her another, very disturbing proposition — which she had turned down.

★★★★★

Now, at the breakfast table, the conversation continued. Aditi put her elbows on the dining table and gave Shoma one of her pained looks.

'Well, for someone who lives here you are a total ignoramus, that's for sure. You can't even name ten birds that can be found here. You wouldn't know what a crow was if it announced its name to you!' She turned to her brother. 'You know those paradise flycatchers are nesting somewhere near the gully? One of them nearly flew down to my feet!'

Shoma flushed red. 'Well, one thing I do know is that you bird people are really silly. Who in their right minds would name a bird "paradise flycatcher"? The first thing you would expect in paradise is that at least there wouldn't be any flies there! I mean I could understand if it were called 'garbage heap flycatcher' or 'Aditi's mouth flycatcher ...'

'Very droll!' Siddharth said in that belittling tone which always made Shoma want to throw up all over him. He turned to his sister. 'So how many species have we notched up so far?'

'Sixty-three,' she said, 'and we've only been here five days.'

'Five days?' Shoma shook her head incredulously. 'It seems more like five years!'

'Shoma! No need to be rude, dear!' Nani said, a frown creasing her brow. She sighed. Why did it always have to be like this? Why couldn't Shoma be a little nicer to her cousins instead of taking issue with them all the time? Agreed, Siddharth and Aditi could be somewhat tiresome and sometimes did make you want to smack them, but surely Shoma could be a little more understanding. They were her guests, after all.

Poor Brijesh just sat quietly and stared at his plate as he listened to the arguments.

'Sorry, Nani,' Shoma said primly, 'I was only stating the facts as I perceived them!'

'It doesn't matter, Nani,' Siddharth said, smiling with all his beautiful even teeth. 'For some people, ignorance must remain bliss! Forgive her, for she knows not what she says!'

'Okay, children, that's enough.'

Aditi turned to Brijesh, whom she had been eyeing slyly. She thought he was awfully cute. He actually was quite a good-looking boy, with strong, square shoulders, a straight back and nose and firm jaw, neatly trimmed soft black hair and a tanned complexion, and those expressive sad brown eyes.

'Brijesh, do you bird-watch too?' Aditi asked sweetly.

The boy shook his head. 'Uh ... no!' he mumbled.

'You really should, you know,' Aditi said enthusiastically. 'You could come along with us and we'll show you some really beautiful birds. Shoma here certainly won't!'

'Sorry, Aditi!' Shoma said unctuously. 'But I'm taking Brijesh for a cycle ride around the lake this morning.' She smiled dazzlingly at Brijesh. 'Right, Brijesh?' Actually, she had just blurted this out. Till a moment ago, she had had no intention of taking Brijesh anywhere, but come what may Aditi had to be thwarted! She soldiered on recklessly. 'Hey, can I call you Bridge?'

Brijesh looked embarrassed. 'Uh-huh,' he mumbled again, 'If you like!'

'Great!' Shoma said, 'And you can call me Budgie, like Nani does!'

It struck her that 'Budgie and Bridge' sounded quite cool. It made them sound like outlaw partners (like Butch

Cassidy and the Sundance Kid) shooting down saintly bird-watchers in some badass Western movie! But the poor guy had such sad brown eyes; like Djinn's when he was being scolded.

'Siddharth, how many species have we made recordings for?' Aditi asked, though of course, she knew.

'Fifty-one, and papa has photographs of all of them, so our presentation should be great!'

'Well, maybe we can get a few more before the seminar – there's still a week left.'

'That's what I'm hoping.'

'Oh God, so that means you bird freaks will be stampeding around the place like a herd of buffalos for another week?' Shoma shook her head again. 'Why can't you have your jamborees elsewhere? Like Delhi or Bombay? Why does it have to be right here?'

That was the icing on the cake. Nani had agreed to accommodate some of the participants of the seminar, which was to be held at the Mehegtal Resort just outside Mehegtal town. Shoma thought her peace of mind—in fact, her whole life—would be turned upside down for an entire week. While the 'formal' part of the seminar was only for four days, crackpot bird-watchers would begin arriving a few days earlier and maybe even stay on afterwards. So, there would be wackos stomping all over the house and surrounding forests, fluffing up the egos of Siddharth and Aditi, who would think they were the hosts and personally responsible for every bird that was spotted … Well, maybe she should 'hijack' Brijesh after all and show him around; hopefully he wouldn't be anything like Aditi and Siddharth. But then he lived in Mumbai and would probably have a panic attack if he saw a spider.

'This is not a jamboree,' Aditi was saying now. 'It's a very important international seminar. It's a great honour for papa and Siddharth to be invited to make a presentation and for Nani to host some of the distinguished participants.'

'Hah! All you people do is trample about the place like drunken bears, making excited noises when you see something, and write lists and then give long boring lectures and eat and drink and fight over whether it was this bird or that. Give me a break!'

'I believe I'm one of the youngest participants to have been invited to present a paper,' Siddharth said smugly, giving Shoma a withering look.

'Yeah, and dumbest!'

'Shoma! Apologize to Siddharth. And stop all this bickering, please! What will poor Brijesh think?'

'Nani, but it's true! And why should one apologize for what is true?'

'Budgie, please don't argue with me. You're beginning to give me a headache.'

'She gives everyone a headache!' Siddharth said.

'Certainly, to people who deserve one!'

'Shoma, did you hear what I said?'

'But Nani!'

'Good morning all. And what is the argument about, dare I ask?'

They all looked up from the breakfast table, as Siddharth and Aditi's parents walked in. Both were dressed in khakis – in jackets and trousers which seemed to be entirely composed of pockets and zips. Sohan Uncle put down his camera with its huge lens and tripod and rubbed his hands. He was a big-built, balding man with thick spectacles, thick lips and a heavy bear-like way of shambling. He had made a lot of money opening a chain of grocery stores in England. Vinita Aunty put down two pairs of large, powerful binoculars. Like Siddharth, she had slightly protruding, very white teeth, and a face which, Shoma thought, had been filched from a billy-goat, complete with slightly bulging stone-colored eyes. The only thing missing was the goatee!

'Papa, I had a red-billed leiothrix down by the lake!' Siddharth said excitedly.

'Here we go again …' Shoma sang, rolling her eyes.

'Oh, that's great,' said Sohan Uncle. 'Did you get a recording?'

'Yes, of course! Very clear too.'

'Good man!'

'And papa, I had these paradise flycatchers this morning,' Aditi added. 'They nearly touched my feet! We told Shoma, but imagine, she lives here and hasn't seen any of them.'

Shoma gave a hollow groan and they all looked at her. Vinita Aunty's eyebrows shot up inquiringly.

'What?' she asked in her whispery voice which everyone else thought sounded so posh. 'Did you say something, Shoma?'

'Um, no ...'

'Oh, did someone pull a flush then?' Siddharth asked, winking at Aditi. They all laughed. Brijesh just stared at his rolled oats.

Shoma, who was sitting next to Siddharth, thrust her face into his.

'Very ... droll!' she mimicked him perfectly and pushed back her chair. 'Nani, I'm done, may I be excused, please?'

At the head of the table, Nani sighed and nodded. 'Okay, very well, dear ...'

'Thank you!'

She vacated her place with alacrity and left the room. From the corner of her eye she saw the whole hateful family (except Nani and Brijesh, of course) shake their heads at each other in mock concern and smile knowingly, as if at a loss as to how to deal with someone as delinquent as her. The tears were pricking now, and that made her even angrier. She stopped in the doorway, hidden by the curtain. They were sure to start talking about her now. She was right.

'You know, Nani, Shoma really ought to take up bird-watching or something useful,' Aditi said as if she were forty-five years old and not fourteen.

'She lives in this beautiful place and sees nothing! What a waste.' That was the pious Siddharth.

'Pity her parents haven't encouraged her,' Vinita Aunty said. She shook her head and murmured, 'All that Ramona does is flit from one party to another ... such an airhead and social butterfly really.' Shoma's mother, Ramona, was Vinita Aunty's younger sister, and by far the prettier of the two.

'Where are Ramona and Dalbir anyway?'

'Ramona is in Paris, and Dalbir, well I don't really know, Bangalore, I think …' Nani said vaguely.

'No chance of them getting back together?'

Vinita Aunty's eyes were flinty. Many years ago, she had desperately wanted to marry Shoma's father and had almost become engaged to him, but then one day Ramona had waltzed into the room and Dalbir, Shoma's dad, had fallen for her hook, line and sinker and dropped poor Vinita Aunty like a hot potato. Vinita Aunty had never forgiven Ramona for that, and still bore her a grudge, even though she was now secretly happy that Dalbir and Ramona had split up.

'Seems doubtful they'd get back together now,' Nani sighed, 'it's been over five years.'

'You mean Shoma has been living with you for five years?'

'Well, yes. Actually, she's settled down quite well. She likes her school in Mehegtal. And she has Djinn. She's doing all right!'

'Except when we come to visit, then she really becomes impossible.' Siddharth shook his head. 'Nani, how've you managed to remain sane? And that wolf really ought to be in a cage!'

'She's fine if you let her be. She's had a rough time. And she's very fond of painting – watercolours and posters, though she rarely shows me what she's done.'

Vinita Aunty's eyebrows shot up again. 'What? I can't imagine someone like her using watercolours; they're far too delicate … But she does need to learn some manners and social graces. And she's got such a sharp tongue. She really must learn to control it.'

Sohan Uncle nodded. 'It's like Aditi said, she really ought to take up something worthwhile. All she does is ride that bicycle of hers all over the place from morning to evening, with that horrible wolf running beside her.'

'Well, she is bit of a free spirit, but I do think that's better than sitting in front of the television all day, or playing video games, don't you agree? And as I said, she does paint rather well – she showed me her paintings once …' Nani paused. 'They were quite violent pictures, though quite good really; she does have talent.'

'Gimme five, Nani!' Shoma exulted silently behind her curtain. When not out birding, Aditi and Siddharth did little else but sit in front of the television set or play video and computer games. One of their chief grouses against Nani's beautiful house was that it didn't have a satellite dish, and of course no wi-fi and internet connection.

'Well, sure … but surely a balance is required,' Sohan Uncle nodded. 'We'll try our best to make her see the error of her ways, but …'

'She's like Ramona,' Vinita Aunty said, shaking her head, 'Stubborn and cheeky. And nothing will change her.'

'Pig-headed!' Aditi said spitefully.

'Aditi, please! That's not a nice thing to say.'

'Sorry, Nani!'

'Okay, guys, are we done here? Let's go out and get some more recordings. Get your equipment. And take the GPS too.'

'Sure, papa!'

Vinita Aunty smiled dazzlingly at Brijesh.

'Would you like to join us, dear?'

Poor Brijesh looked like he was caught between a rock and a hard place. Nani caught on at once.

'Umm … I think Shoma's invited him to go for a bike ride with her,' she told Vinita Aunty. 'Maybe next time!'

Brijesh looked hugely relieved. Behind her curtain, Shoma looked miffed. Why couldn't he have spoken up for himself? Why did Nani have to rescue him? Then she remembered that his mom had just died and his dad was a drunk and he was here in the midst of quarrelling strangers! He must have been mega-embarrassed, poor guy!

The family rose from the table and Shoma vanished like smoke up the stairs to her room. She looked out of the window. The sunlight through the trees and over the meadow and the lake was gauzy and sandy gold. It was still and prickly. She knew it would be pouring within a couple of hours. The far mountains were already shrouded by an opalescent ivory haze. So, should she take her sketch-pad and paints and go for a bike ride with Djinn? (She had no intention of taking Brijesh along – she had made the offer just to snub Aditi!)

Her scarlet and black mountain bike and her bright green fiberglass boat were her pride and joy. The mountain bike had twelve gears and was light and sturdy, with knobbly tyres which could grip the most pebbly and gravelly of surfaces. She'd taken it virtually everywhere – almost right around the lake (the to-and-fro trip was 18.86 kilometres, according to its speedometer!); up and down the winding forest tracks that led up to the mountains; and even along the high narrow ridges from where you could see two valleys at the same time. She always wore her yellow helmet and knee- and arm-pads when she biked, because it was all too easy to be tossed off when you came careening down a narrow mountain track and missed seeing a deviously placed rock or skidded on pine needles or went around a bend too fast. When it was too steep or otherwise impossible to ride the bike, it was light enough that she could simply carry it on her slim but sturdy shoulders. She nodded. She would go biking. She'd take her heavy-duty raincoat of course. It would be fun splashing through huge puddles and impromptu streams as she raced downhill, trying desperately not to skid. So much better than peering up into the pine and oak trees with binoculars, arguing about what you saw and 'having' this bird or that. She watched as the Vermas set out, noting with satisfaction that none of them was carrying rain gear – but they did have a lot of their very expensive equipment. They really were very stupid, and considering they lived in England where it rained all the time, doubly so. In the hills and mountains here, it was de rigueur that you carried at least umbrellas whenever you set out!

The question arose, surprising herself: should she warn them? She'd love them to come back looking like drowned rats, but the stuff they were carrying was worth a lot of money. Sohan Uncle's Nikons with their huge lenses, Vinita Aunty's Leica spotting scope, their binoculars and the recording equipment that Siddharth and Aditi so proudly strutted around with. And she liked such things: they were so beautiful and precision-made. The lenses shone, reflecting mysterious purples and blues and mauves, and someone had taken great care in designing and finishing them. They were beautiful in themselves and beauty in any form appealed to her.

She leaned out of her window.

'Sohan Uncle ...' she called.

He looked up, as did the rest of his family.

'Oh, Shoma? What? You want to apologize? That's okay ...'

She gulped and shook her head. 'It's going to rain. Your things will get wet ...'

'Rain?' They all looked up. 'Nonsense, my dear! The sky's clear and the sun's out! No chance of rain.'

'And anyway, this isn't England after all,' Aditi said smartly and they all laughed.

'Still nice of you to warn us, dear,' Vinita Aunty said. Perhaps the girl could still be salvaged. Well, they had a whole month to try ...

'Would you and Brijesh like to join us?' Aditi invited, in a tone implying they would be doing her a monumental favor.

'No.'

'So nice of you to apologize,' Aditi went on smarmily, 'we understand.'

Shoma shut her window and withdrew, taking a deep breath. Well, it was their funeral, though it would be a pity if all that snazzy equipment got ruined.

2

As soon as they had left, Shoma went down again, warily looking out for Brijesh. If only she could avoid him and Nani and sneak out with her bike. She knew Djinn would be snoozing in the sun in the verandah. He was, but so was Brijesh! He was sitting in one of the rocking chairs and staring at the view. Djinn lay peaceably nearby, his wise brown eyes occasionally glancing at Brijesh, before he shut them with a sigh. Shoma paused in the doorway looking at Brijesh. Was that the glimmer of tears in his eyes? He had extraordinarily long eyelashes, she noticed. Djinn saw her, wagged his tail briefly and continued to snooze. Crap! There was no way she and Djinn could escape unseen!

'Um … hi Bridge!' Shoma said tentatively. Brijesh rocked back, startled, and then looked at her, quickly rubbing his eyes.

'Um … hi!' He glanced at Djinn and then at her.

'Do you like dogs?' Shoma asked, 'Or are you scared of him?'

Brijesh glanced at Djinn. 'He's a ferocious-looking fellow, isn't he?' he said admiringly, 'I would like to be friends with him … if that's possible, but he is a powerful chap!' Shoma immediately warmed up to him.

'Ya, he is! You know, he once attacked a leopard in our school who was just about to pounce on the Head Girl!' she said.

'What? Wow!'

Proudly, she recounted the incident. Maybe she ought to invite him for a bike ride. If he didn't want to come, no one could say she hadn't asked, and if he did … well, maybe it wouldn't be so bad after all.

'So, would you like to come for a bike ride?' she asked. 'It's going to rain in about an hour or so, but it'll still be fun!'

'Okay …'

'Great. You'll have to use Nana's old bike. It's also a mountain bike but I think we may first have to pump up its tyres.'

They went over to the bicycle shed, where she pulled out the dusty bicycle and rummaged around for the pump.

'Here, I'll do it!' Brijesh offered as she fixed the pump's nozzle to the bike's tyre valve.

'Thanks!'

She watched as he pumped up the tyre effortlessly.

'Do you like hiking and trekking and mountain climbing?' she asked.

'Yes. Mom and I loved trekking but I don't get much of a chance to do many outdoor things in Mumbai. But I swim a lot, both in pools and the sea! And I like aero-modelling.'

'Oh. I can't swim very well. Nani says I only dog paddle!' she admitted. Suddenly she smiled prettily. 'Hey, maybe I could take you on hikes and treks and rides and teach you how to climb mountains and you can teach me how to swim properly! Deal?'

For the first time, a shy smile lit up his face.

'Deal!' he said softly as Nani came down into the garden. She smiled too — at least her fiery little granddaughter had made friends with this poor sad boy.

'Hi Nani! I'm taking Bridge for a bike ride around the lake!'

'Okay, dear. Don't do too much: he needs to acclimatize to the altitude first …'

'Nani, he's fine! Look, he pumped up both those tyres in no time!'

Brijesh hadn't brought a raincoat so Shoma rummaged around the bicycle shed a little more and pulled out Nana's old brown one from a battered tin trunk.

'We'll just dust this down first,' she said, 'it's full of cobwebs!'

'Are you sure it's going to rain?' Brijesh asked.

'Ya … see, it's all prickly and still and there's this haze … it means rain is on its way. Okay, let's go! Djinn, come on boy!'

They bumped down the track leading to the path around the lake, skirting the meadow, Djinn keeping pace easily beside them.

'Isn't this great?' she yelled exultantly, her frizzy ponytail bouncing madly, her face aglow. It felt so nice to actually have someone biking beside her; someone to chat to.

Brijesh just nodded, focusing on the rocky path ahead. Beyond the meadow, they entered the pine and oak forest again, and the path began to climb.

'We can actually bike up this if we use the right gear!' Shoma said. They reached the top of the slope and stopped to catch their breath. Voices floated up from the bottom of the slope on the other side, up ahead.

Shoma grinned mischievously. 'It's Siddharth and Aditi and their parents,' she whispered. 'Let's give them a fright! Follow me!'

She sailed down, pedalling furiously to build up speed. Brijesh followed tentatively and then began enjoying himself as his bike gained momentum too. Behind him, Big Djinn followed, in complete silence.

'Yohooo! Gangway! Incoming!' Shoma yelled at the top of her voice as she hurtled past the startled bird-watchers, ringing her bell furiously. Brijesh followed close behind, his eyes glued to the path ahead. Djinn just loped behind them.

'Shoma!' Vinita Aunty squealed, jumping into a bush as Aditi nearly fell into the lake with fright and Siddharth uttered a panic-stricken, 'Yaaa!' Sohan Uncle almost toppled his tripod over.

'That girl really needs a good spanking!' Vinita Aunty exclaimed angrily, picking herself out of the rather nettle-covered bush. 'Ma is just too lenient with her. And now she's corrupting that poor boy! She's going to turn him into a delinquent too!'

'It's her mother who ought to be taking care of her,' Sohan Uncle said disapprovingly.

'That Ramona!' Vinita Aunty said pityingly. 'She's going to mess up her life good and proper one of these days. And poor Ma will be left looking after this hellion child forever!'

'Maybe,' Siddharth said in his saintly way. 'Maybe when all these expert birders come they could influence her and make her take it up, or do something worthwhile. She'll be in such exalted and distinguished company ...'

Aditi shook her head scornfully. 'Not Shoma – all she'll do is ride that horrible bike all over their toes, if I know her.'

'Okay, kids – hear that, quiet now! Siddharth, switch on your mike ...' Sohan Uncle scanned a thick patch of lantana, from where some unseen bird piped and whistled sweetly.

Rattling ahead on their bikes, Shoma and Brijesh slowed down, glancing back.

'Was that fun or what?' Shoma gloated, her cheeks pink. 'Did you see? Aditi nearly fell into the lake!'

Brijesh looked like he was trying to hold back a grin.

'So ... er ... you don't like bird-watching?' he asked.

Shoma shook her head vigorously. 'No, I like birds but I don't like to bird-watch the way they do! Making long lists and fighting over whether it was this bird or that and who saw it first and who has the longest list. I just like to paint and draw them sometimes.' A dreadful thought occurred to her: 'What about you? Do you like birds and bird-watching?'

He looked thoughtful. 'Um ... I like different kinds of birds – airplanes!' he said. 'I love making remote-control models.'

'Oh! Wow!' She paused. Then, shyly: 'See, I'll show you!'

From her bicycle's carrier, she removed a flat canvas satchel from which she extracted a drawing pad. She handed it to him. Brijesh flipped it open.

'Oh!' he said surprised, turning the pages slowly. 'Wow! They ... they look so alive!'

'You think so?' She was pleased.

'Do you know what they are?'

'Nah, and I don't care. What does it matter? See, there are some other paintings of the lake ... Come, I'll take you to a spot where you get a fabulous view! It's on top of the ridge, so you can see the house and lake on one side and the road leading to the house from Mehegtal town on the other. Come on, we have to go up this path. It gets a bit steep so we'll have to push our bikes.'

The pebbly path ran alongside a stream that tinkled its way down to the lake.

'We can freewheel down this on our way back!' Shoma said. 'It's great fun. Sometimes you can go straight into the lake if you don't brake in time!'

They were both panting by the time they reached the ridge top.

'It's almost level from here on,' Shoma said. 'Just follow that narrow path through the trees.'

Tall pines fringed the ridge top, a narrow game-trail running through them. They both got on their bicycles and began pedalling again, back in the direction of the house. The path climbed a bit and then ended abruptly at the edge of a deep ravine. The drop was sheer.

'This is the place,' Shoma said. 'From this side you can see the place where the donkeys' stables and car park are and the road leading up to it. And from here, you can see the meadow and lake and the house itself. We climbed up the ridge from a path that's on the other side of this gully.'

They put down their bicycles and sat on rocks looking at the view, with Djinn settling down between them. Shoma glanced at Brijesh. He was resting his chin on his knees and staring ahead. She was used to being on her own and once again realized that it was nice to have someone along – someone you could share stuff with.

'I guess you don't have any brothers and sisters?' she asked. He shook his head.

'No, me neither.' She made a face. 'Except those horrible cousins! You should get a dog, you know. Then you won't be alone! Djinn comes along with me everywhere.'

His face became stony. 'Papa hates dogs,' he replied tonelessly. 'He doesn't care for anyone or anything except his booze!'

'Does your mom like dogs?' Too late she remembered. 'Oops, I'm sorry!' She buried a hand in Djinn's thick fur to commiserate.

He gulped. 'You know, he never came to see her in hospital ... I used to go there after school every day and he never visited once!' His Adam's apple wobbled.

'Oh, I'm sorry! Even mama and papa keep fighting. That's why I'm with Nani. You know, Nani likes rescuing people like us! She even rescued Djinn!'

He glanced at her and grinned wanly, but his eyes were brimming over. He wiped them impatiently and then he pointed across the lake. 'What's that horrible building across there?'

'That's a new posh golfing resort built by some very rich dude who is friends with the Prime Minister. There's a golf course on the mountaintop. You know, they cut all the trees on the slope and then built a sort of wall out of mud and rocks, till it was level with the ridge top. Nani says they're waiting for a day when some minister is free and will come and open it.'

'Oh,' he said. She glanced at him again.

'How ... how did you get that black eye and bruised cheek?' she asked. 'Did you get into a fight or something?' He fingered his face gently.

'Papa ...' he whispered so softly she barely heard him. 'After ... after he had smashed nearly every one of my model airplanes with my cricket bat!'

'Oh God! But ... but why ... was he mad or something?'

Brijesh shrugged. 'Who knows and who cares? He just barged into the room and laid about with the bat ... and then hit me ... I had barely brought mom's ashes back home ...' He was crying now, but managed to control himself. 'Sorry!' he said, 'Sorry!'

'It's okay,' she said, utterly appalled.

'I ... I only managed to save one plane – a Lancaster bomber that I had nearly finished making. I kicked it under the bed.'

'But that's terrible!' And no wonder Nani had taken off like a bat out of hell to rescue him!

Just then, they heard the faint rumble of thunder like distant artillery far away across the northern mountains.

'I told you it's going to rain!' Shoma said, wanting to change the subject and feeling vindicated, 'In another twenty minutes maybe!'

'Looks like it!' He glanced at her again. She was a slim, wiry little thing, reaching up to his chin, with glossy limbs honey-browned by the sun, a round, cheerful face, rosy pink cheeks and frizzy dark brown hair, tied up in a high ponytail. Her eyes were dark brown and sparkled and her small pink ears jutted out just a little too much, rather like scallop shells, her nose was cutely snub, with a tiny sparkling diamond resting snug in it. She was wearing tough denim overalls (which gave away a little more than just the gentlest hint of soft, rounded curves beneath), over a red top and a red baseball cap.

From far below, the sound of some idiot's horn wafted up from the Mehegtal road. They looked down; a big, silver

SUV was nosing its way through a flock of wobbly sheep, its horn blaring. They watched it as it climbed up and eventually came to a halt in the Cloud-house car park.

'Uh-oh, it looks like some of those bird freaks have already arrived!' Shoma said.

She was right: two adults and two kids climbed out of the vehicle.

'The hostiles have landed!' Shoma announced. She smiled beautifully and mimicked Vinita Aunty perfectly: 'Don't worry, Aditi darling, you're prettier than all of them!' Then she hunkered down and gave Brijesh a running commentary of what she saw.

'One female, one male and my God, two snotty kids … Female is short and dumpy and wearing a very rumpled baggy shirt and khaki cargos. She's strutting around, with big binos around her neck and has a very big bum and her hands on her hips. Meatloaf, that's what she is. Male is in a very tight T-shirt and jeans, with a belt bag like a holster. He has very short hair, like American soldiers. He's taking out stuff from the back of the car …'

She turned her attention to the kids. 'One boy, gawky with glasses and red splotched face – does he have pimples or what. Zit-face. Girl, mousy looking, is clutching GI's belt, quite fair – skinny. Bony Mouse of course! Boring …'

Brijesh glanced at her and grinned quietly.

The breeze had picked up suddenly. Sailing over the lake, the advance guard of clouds made good time, a silvery curtain of rain preceding them.

'Raincoats on!' Shoma announced gleefully as they quickly shrugged into them and she stuffed her precious sketch-pad into its waterproof case.

'Here you go, Djinn!' Shoma took the dog's bright yellow raincoat from her bicycle basket and put it on the dog. He just stood there quietly, rumbling softly.

As the mists began shrouding the lake, it took on an eerie, silvery shimmer, as if at any moment some ghostly monster of the deep would erupt, snapping its enormous jaws and exhaling toxic vapours. Shoma studied the effect. She'd have to memorize the scene and go home and paint it.

All too soon, the rain attained a steady roar.

'We'd better go now!' Shoma told Brijesh. 'It might stop in twenty minutes or go on for three days!' They got on their bicycles and rattled slowly back along the ridge till they reached the path going down to the lake.

'Be careful, it can get very slippery!' she cautioned as they bumped down. Once on the lake path, they picked up speed, splashing through the puddles and slush, their faces pink with exhilaration, enjoying the feel of the water spraying up from under their wheels. Djinn just cantered along happily. At the door, Nani greeted them anxiously.

'Budgie, where are the others? They really ought not to have gone out. Their guests have arrived. Now you both come in and dry off!'

'They went on their own, Nani. We weren't with them …'

'Have they taken umbrellas?'

'No, Nani,' she said as piously as Siddharth ever could have. 'I told them to, but they said it wouldn't rain …'

'Oh, they'll be soaked and cold!'

'And all their valuable equipment will get spoiled …'

'And Kusum and Annie have gone to the market, so I can't send the two after them.'

'Nani,' Shoma went on virtuously, 'I think they've gone on the path along the lake. We could ride after them with umbrellas and zip lock bags for their equipment …'

'But dear, it's raining so heavily and you're both already soaked to the skin!'

'Nani, we have our raincoats on. We're dry!'

'Oh well, okay – there's no point having them all come down with pneumonia.'

Shoma grabbed a few big zip lock bags, a spare raincoat and three folding umbrellas, including a ghastly candy-floss pink one, stuffing them into both their bikes' baskets.

'Nani, I'll take a towel too. Put it in my knapsack.' She dumped her paints and sketch-pad on the table and shouldered her waterproof knapsack. 'Should we take some hot cocoa for them too?' she asked, smiling angelically.

'You really are very sweet and considerate when you want to be, dear! I'll keep some ready for them here.' Nani gazed at her fondly, remembering the frightened little girl that had come to live with her nearly five years ago. Gradually she had gained confidence, and had begun exploring on her own. Maybe her bike and even the boat had been inspired gifts from her father, giving her the confidence and freedom to roam further afield, and now she spent nearly all of her time outdoors. And then there was Big Djinn, who was really a godsend.

'Nani, the towel is to dry all their cameras and binoculars, not them,' Shoma clarified.

'Go on, dear. And be careful, both of you.'

'Wait a sec!' Shoma shot off indoors and up to her room. She was down in minutes, carrying a battery-powered revolving red light and small siren. She clipped them on to the handlebars of her bike and grinned at Brijesh. 'Drowned rats rescue team setting forth,' she sang, switching on the light and siren, as Nani shook her head and tried not to laugh.

It was certainly thundering down when they finally came upon the Vermas, about a kilometre down the lake path beyond the stream. They were sheltering miserably under a huge tree, huddled over their precious equipment. They stared in her direction, watching the flashes of her light through the pines and listening to the wailing of her siren.

'Shoma!' Sohan Uncle exclaimed as she skidded to a halt besides them, her eyes sparkling. She noted with immense satisfaction that Aditi and Siddharth really did look like drowned pink rats. Aditi's hair was hanging stringily down her face and Siddharth's teeth were chattering.

'Wipe your stuff with this and put them in the bags and then wrap the towel around them!' she barked, handing the towel over, as if she were responding to an emergency SOS.

'C…c…could I wipe my face?' Siddharth sniffled, as Aditi nodded, 'Me too, please!'

'What a country!' Vinita Aunty said bitterly. 'They can't even forecast the weather properly. In England, they would have told us exactly what it was going to be like …'

'I told you it would rain, but you didn't listen!'

'You!' Aditi spat uncharitably. 'What do you know?'

'I know that I'm the one wearing the raincoat and you're the one looking like a drowned pink rat, so there!'

'Pink rat? Mama, she called me a drowned pink rat!'

'Okay, is that all the stuff?' Both their baskets were really overflowing and mountain bikes normally didn't have carriers or baskets. But Nana had also installed a tiny seat behind his saddle to accommodate her when she had been little, and both the bicycles had large baskets up front.

'You can put some stuff in my knapsack too, it's waterproof!' she offered sweetly. 'Okay, we'll see you all at the house, bye!'

Aditi played her ace. 'Er … Brijesh, can I ride on the little seat behind you please?' she asked, making big innocent eyes at the boy.

Taken completely by surprise, Brijesh shrugged. 'Er … whatever, if you like …' he mumbled as Shoma flushed angrily. She watched as Aditi squeaked a thank you and Brijesh stood stoically as she climbed on behind him.

'You know he's not supposed to exert himself. He has to get used to the altitude!' Shoma exclaimed.

'Dear, you've been making him ride up and down all these slopes – I'm sure he's fine and Aditi doesn't weigh very much!' Vinita Aunty said.

'Well, if he faints don't blame me!' Shoma yelled. 'Come on, Bridge, let's go!' They wobbled off heroically as the rest of the family straggled behind with their umbrellas. Aditi leaned forward and clasped her hands around Brijesh's waist, clutching on to him tightly and resting her chin on his shoulder. She thought he was really cute. Brijesh just stared stonily ahead and pedalled steadily.

Shoma reached the house first and disembarked, hoisting her bike up the verandah steps as Brijesh and Aditi wobbled up. Aditi smiled slyly to herself and thrust her cheek against Brijesh's as Shoma looked at them, her eyes flashing angrily.

Brijesh stared straight ahead as he stopped the bike and put his feet down.

'Er ... you can get off now!' he muttered.

At the house, the new arrivals had all freshened up and were sitting in the drawing room, as Nani bustled about organizing tea. Shoma pushed her bike into the deep verandah, took off her raincoat and shook out her ponytail. She took Djinn's raincoat off and rubbed him down with a towel. He wagged his tail stiffly in acknowledgement, then curled up on the rug by the rocking chair. Shoma began carefully unloading the equipment and laid it all out on a table in the hall. Brijesh dragged his bike up the steps as Aditi made an attempt to help, staring meaningfully into his eyes.

She now knew exactly how to bug the heck out of her bratty cousin – and she was going to enjoy herself doing so.

'We're back, Nani,' Shoma called, 'and the others are on their way.'

'Dry yourself off, Budgie, or you'll catch a chill …'

Tentatively Shoma entered the drawing room, followed by Brijesh and Aditi. Nani looked up from pouring out tea for the guests.

'This is my granddaughter Shoma,' she told them, smiling fondly at Shoma. 'And that's Brijesh, the son of a student of mine. Aditi, of course, you all know! Dears, have you dried off? Say hello – that's Arvind and Kalpana, and their dad Professor Damodar, and Charulata Aunty.'

'H…hello …' Shoma murmured as Brijesh just mumbled something under his breath. Aditi greeted Arvind and Kalpana with an effusive 'Hi, guys, great to see you!'

'So, Shoma, I see Aditi's taken you birding even in this weather!' Professor Damodar boomed, indicating the binoculars that she had taken out from her backpack and that were still dangling from her hands. 'What did you see?'

'We had four wet pink rats,' Shoma said before she could stop herself, giggling. Nani looked up sharply.

Then she said, 'Shoma dear, you'll be sleeping in my room. I've given your room to Arvind and Kalpana …'

Professor Damodar brayed again, 'You see, my dear, they can't sleep with me. They say I snore too loudly. My own children!'

'But … but …' Her room! Her beloved room! And Nani had just given it away to these freaks without even asking her. She swallowed.

Just then there was the sound of shuffling footsteps in the verandah outside and a rumble from Djinn. The others had arrived.

Within seconds, they had all fallen on the guests with great cries of delight. Sohan Uncle went from one to another, shaking hands vigorously. Vinita Aunty looked earnestly at Meatloaf and made some disparaging remark about weather forecasting in India. 'I really must get out of these wet things,' she tinkled, and Siddharth enthusiastically greeted Arvind and Kalpana, whom they obviously knew from before. 'Yup, absolutely filthy weather and they didn't even know it was going to rain,' Siddharth told Kalpana, staring at her disconcertingly.

'Hey, you guys, we have a new recruit!' Aditi said blithely, pulling Brijesh forward. 'Meet Brijesh! He's dead keen to begin bird-watching, so we have our work cut out for us! We'll take him along whenever we go!'

Poor Brijesh didn't know what had hit him as the others made approving, welcoming noises.

'You know, we've had seventy-five species so far, including paradise flycatchers and leiothrixes,' Aditi went on. 'When the sun's out, it's really quite good for birding.'

Quietly, Shoma backed out and went up to her room, where two hateful blue overnighters were parked. She kicked

47

them and flung herself down on her bed. Then she heard
Nani's voice float up to her.

'Budgie, will you bring down some more towels
please ...'

It was going to be a tough week ahead.

3

It was awful. By that afternoon, Arvind, Kalpana, Siddharth and Aditi had taken complete possession of her room. They were sitting on her bed, with Siddharth feeling very important as he played back his recordings and showed them slides on his laptop. Worse, Aditi had dragged Brijesh in with them and had assumed the role of his personal bird-watching coach.

Before they had taken over her room, Shoma had quickly removed most of her 'valuables' – her paints, crayons, pencils, sketch pens, rotrings, which were special pens for making pen and ink sketches, and of course her sketch-pads. She staggered out with them, wondering where to put them. In the end, she dumped them on Nani's dressing table.

'You can put them in the storeroom, dear, at least for the time being,' Nani told her, and she bit her lip. So now her precious things were being relegated to the 'godown', which is what Kusum called the storeroom. Well, maybe she would go and live there too! No one would miss her anyway. Even that stupid Brijesh was closeted away with the others.

'So, Shoma, Siddharth and Aditi say you're not too keen on birds,' Professor Damodar said, smiling at her at the lunch table.

'Uh-uh ...' she murmured, shaking her head, 'I'm allergic actually.'

'Shoma just likes riding her bike like a lunatic, scaring all the wildlife and birdlife for miles around!' Aditi said in her smarmy way.

'Yeah, and if I didn't ride my bike you would all still be huddling under that tree like drowned rats and all your fancy equipment would have gotten ruined!'

'Shoma, dear ...'

'Well, it is true!'

'Where did you get that ridiculous red light and siren from?' Siddharth asked pityingly, forgetting how wet and miserable he had been and how relieved he had felt when he first heard the siren and saw the flashing red light and thought the police had come to rescue them. 'Really, it was such a spectacle!'

'But Shoma, my dear, that's just terrible; you live in such a lovely place. Surely you must have noticed some of the beautiful birds around?' Meatloaf sounded shocked. She had a penetrating plangent voice, rather like the blare of a wedding band's trumpet, Shoma thought.

'No!' Shoma said stubbornly. 'I haven't noticed them and I won't!'

'Well, we'll just have to make you then, won't we – you don't know what you're missing!' Meatloaf laughed like a mule braying. 'With all of us around, you won't have a chance to escape! See, young Brijesh here has already started showing an interest, Aditi tells me. And he's hardly been here for a day or so!'

'You should attend some of the sessions of the seminar,' Professor Damodar said seriously, nodding. 'They'll be very instructive.'

'So, what is it that you *do* like doing?' Meatloaf asked her.

'Riding my bike … sai—' Shoma shut up promptly. The existence of *Rubadubdub* must remain a secret. She had hidden her boat deep in the reeds on the shoreline where the meadow gave way to the forest. She smiled charmingly and added, 'I also rescue drowned rats!' But why the heck were they all getting on her case like this? Why couldn't they leave her alone? She wished she could just walk out and curl up with Djinn in the verandah.

'Shoma, there's no need to be rude!' Vinita Aunty spoke sharply.

'Shoma likes to draw and paint, don't you, Budgie?' Nani said benignly.

'Well, birds would be the perfect subject for you then,' Meatloaf said, as if the matter had been settled and that Shoma would henceforth only paint birds. 'Maybe the kids can show you pictures and you can paint them. That would be a nice way to start, don't you think?'

'Never!' Shoma shook her ponytail vigorously.

'What do you like to draw?' Kalpana asked with feigned interest.

'Umm ... pictures ... anything ... things happening ... things that I feel ... Djinn ...'

'Hey, listen!' Siddharth butted in, cocking his head. 'I think the rain's stopped. And that was *Myophonus caeruleus,* the blue whistling thrush, singing ...' He got up from the table. 'Come along, I'll get my mike,' he said and made off. Aditi got up too. 'Come on, Brijesh!' she said, taking his arm and pulling him along. 'You have to hear this properly!' Arvind and Kalpana followed.

'Why don't you go along with them, Shoma?' Meatloaf bared her teeth again. 'Go on, now!'

'I haven't finished my gajar ka halwa,' Shoma said sweetly, loading her bowl with another helping. Brijesh, she thought angrily, could go to hell! Allowing himself to be dragged about by that awful Aditi!

'Nani, why did you give my room to Zit-face and Bony Mouse?' Shoma asked, as she lay beside her grandmother shortly after lunch, flipping through a Calvin and Hobbes book. The rain had stopped but the clouds were still misty over the lake and drifting through the trees in their silent, wispy way. But to the west, shafts of sunlight were streaming out from behind the clouds – in an hour or so it would be brilliantly clear again, everything diamond-bright with raindrops.

'To whom?'

'Oh, what's his name ... that Arvind and his sister?'

'Budgie, you really shouldn't call people names like that – it's not polite.'

'I was not being polite,' Shoma said truthfully and grinned.

'Dear! Well, they said they couldn't sleep in the same room with their father because he snores so I had to give them a room of their own, and yours was the only one left. I have a booking for the remaining room. Sorry, dear, but it's only for a few days. Would you like to sleep with them too? We can put a mattress on the floor if you like …'

'No way! Not with those bird freaks. Their morning alarm probably goes off like a chicken having its throat cut!'

'Maybe you should try to become interested in birds, dear,' Nani suggested pacifically. 'Brijesh seems to be developing an interest already, which is so nice considering everything!'

'Never!' Her eyes flashed. 'I think they should be interested in other things!'

'Oh … like?'

'How should I know? Mountain climbing …'

'Maybe they are.'

'But they never talk about anything else but birds. I'm sick of them!'

'Dear, they've only been here a couple of hours …'

'But Vinita Aunty and the others have been here for so long already.'

'Budgie, you do exaggerate.'

'Well, that's what it feels like!' She waved her hands around expansively. 'I mean, papa and mama don't talk about birds all the time when they come here. Papa talks about racing bikes and speedboats and cool stuff like that, and mama goes on about perfumes and make-up stuff and fancy clothes. They're not gaga over birds – they're normal people!'

Alas, and maybe too busy: they've never had enough time for you, Budgie, have they? Nani thought sadly, reaching out and ruffling Shoma's hair.

'I know, dear. I wish they'd visit more often too, but they're so busy!'

Shoma's eyes gleamed. 'Nani, I got a bike and boat out of papa because he couldn't make it for my last two birthdays. If he doesn't make it for this one, what should I ask him for?'

'I don't know, dear ...'

'I know! I'll ask him for a pup tent and camping equipment. Then I can camp out in the forest with Djinn – it will be so exciting.'

There was a loud knock on the door and Vinita Aunty poked her head around it. 'Ma, it's cleared up, so we're going out. We'll be back around sundown. We've taken flasks of tea and energy bars and fruit.' She spotted Shoma. 'You wouldn't like to join us, would you, Shoma? Brijesh is coming along with us!'

'No thanks, aunty, I have to catch up with my reading ...'

'Oh, I see. Very well then!'

'Take care. Don't get wet again. Take your raincoats!'

'Shoma!'

Vinita Aunty joined the others waiting in the verandah and shook her head. 'She's not coming!'

Charulata (aka Meatloaf) thrust out her jaw aggressively. 'All that girl needs is a little persuasion. Where is she? I'll bring her. Sometimes children just need to be told what to do.'

She stomped into the house and knocked belligerently on Nani's door and barged in.

'Shoma, come along with us! It's such a beautiful afternoon – you can't stay indoors all by yourself! Come on, put on your shoes. We're all waiting in the porch!'

'Yes, why don't you go, Shoma?' Nani said with more hope than she felt.

'No thanks,' Shoma said, going back to her Calvin and Hobbes. 'I have to give this back to the library tomorrow and want to finish it.'

'Don't be silly, dear!' Meatloaf strode over to the bedside and smiled terribly at her.

'What big teeth you have, Meatloaf!' Shoma muttered under her breath, clutching her book in case the woman made a grab for it, 'and what a loud voice, like a wedding band's trumpet!' The woman's eyebrows were raised and her arm was reaching towards her. 'Headmistress?' Shoma blurted suddenly before she could stop herself. 'Miss Trunchbull?'

'What?'

'Er … um … are you a headmistress?' Shoma asked.

'Yes.'

'Bingo! Poor kids.'

'What do you mean? And how did you know?'

'Just like that.'

'Now come along. Put that comic away.'

'No!' She looked up sweetly. 'I have a paper to do on this for school …'

Meatloaf threw up her hands. 'Okay have it your way!' she said, 'Sorry to have disturbed you!' She retreated, smiling a 'well what can one do with a kid like this?' smile.

'Budgie, you really ought to have gone with them. You spend all your time alone here – it's not good,' Nani said reprovingly, but secretly glad that that aggressive woman had gone. 'At least you have some company now and you could show them around.'

'I'm fine, Nani!'

Minutes later, she had slipped off the bed and out of Nani's room. Nani had dozed off and didn't hear her go. Judging by the amount of noise the birders made, it would be easy to follow them, and pretend you were a leopard stalking them. Well, which one of them would she pounce on first?

Vinita Aunty, but only because she needed to be gotten rid of first.

Meatloaf second – because she was an interfering busybody with a very ugly voice. But she would probably be tough and leathery like a mule.

Professor Damodar and Sohan Uncle would make really solid meals; you could keep them in the deep freeze for months, though of course, leopards didn't have deep freezes …

And Siddharth, Aditi, Arvind and Kalpana ... soft, mushy, maggoty perhaps ... Ugh! Junk food! As for Brijesh? He'd probably give her indigestion!

But stalk them she did, silent as a panther, wheeling her bike along, or carrying it if necessary. Of course, Big Djinn came with her. He could move through the trees silent as smoke. There was something thrilling about following people without them being aware of your presence and overhearing what they were talking about, though in this case all they talked about was birds and their stupid seminar and how clever they were for having spotted this rarity or that.

But simply stalking them was not enough. Shoma was a girl of action and it was action she craved. She rummaged in her backpack and took out her pea-shooter. Ah, yes! Now the challenge would be to choose a victim and get up close unseen and then ... pfft!

The birding group was wandering down the lakeside path again, and then up on the path she and Brijesh had taken that morning to the ridge top. They were straggling along loosely, looking and pointing up into the trees and exclaiming excitedly every now and then, though Meatloaf and Vinita Aunty seemed to be gossiping away. The gang of four, accompanied by Brijesh, was being 'led' by Siddharth, who strutted forth pompously as he pointed his mike this way and that. Aditi stayed close to Brijesh, occasionally deliberately bumping into him and murmuring a giggled, 'Oops, sorry!' They stopped to rest in a clearing, beside some fern-covered rocks along the stream that was gurgling down musically. Shoma laid down her bike quietly and wriggled up behind them, Djinn right beside her.

'So, your cousin is not in the least bit interested in birds?' Bony Mouse asked Aditi as the two girls sat down.

'Forget birds, I don't think she's interested in anything at all,' Aditi replied. 'She's beyond help.' She shrugged disparagingly. 'Well, what can you expect? She goes to some primitive gramin paatshala place in that godforsaken little town after all. Her friends must be country bumpkin, village idiot types.'

Bony Mouse giggled.

'So which school do you go to, Brij?' Aditi asked, smiling searchingly at the boy. He mumbled that he attended a school for the specially gifted.

'Oh, wow!' Aditi was impressed. 'I don't think there'll be any country bumpkins and village idiots there!'

'Country bumpkins and village idiots, eh?' Shoma muttered angrily, lying down flat in the wet moss. She put a pebble, small and round as a ball-bearing, into her pea-shooter and drew bead.

Pfft!

And again: *Pfft!*

'Owwww!' Aditi shot up with a squeal, slapping the back of her soft pink neck. 'Something stung me!'

'Owwwch!' Bony Mouse leapt up. 'Something bit me too!'

Already Shoma was wriggling back, grinning gleefully and thankful for the thick lantana hiding her, even though everyone said it was ruining the hills. Now, for Vinita Aunty and Meatloaf ...

She hit Meatloaf smartly on her big bottom and then caused Vinita Aunty to squeal like a pig as a pebble rapped her ear.

'Bullseye!' Shoma murmured delightedly, one hand in Djinn's thick fur. She peered through the twiggy mesh of lantana at her victims.

And to her horror, she found Brijesh looking straight at her! She'd been rumbled! Oh crap, he would surely let the cat out of the bag and she would be in trouble! Nani would be really angry! She glared at him but he stared back at her expressionlessly, giving no indication that he had actually seen her. In fact, Shoma thought angrily, maybe he had looked right through her. Maybe all he was seeing was Aditi!

Aditi was now leaning towards him and coyly asking him: 'Brijesh, please, could you see if there's a sting or anything on my neck? Something just stung me!' She had taken his hand and was guiding his fingers to the targeted spot.

'Here! Ouch, it still hurts!'

Shoma knew she really ought to be backing away out of sight, but she watched, transfixed. Brijesh glanced at Aditi's neck.

'No,' he muttered, 'there's no sting!'

Thankfully, he didn't glance in Shoma's direction again.

The birding party began moving ahead. Shoma picked up her bike and decided she'd done enough stalking and pea-shooting for the day. She wondered if Brijesh would keep his counsel, or ultimately tell Aditi what he had seen. Oh well, it had been worth it! She got onto her bike and bumped down the slope and rode homewards, Djinn at her heels.

The birding party returned shortly before dusk, tired and excited by the birds they had spotted. They dumped their equipment onto the big verandah table and flopped down in the comfortable armchairs, waiting for Kusum to bring them tea.

'Imagine, Nani, we had 48 species just this afternoon!' Aditi said excitedly. 'And Brijesh is becoming so good already – he had seen the speckled piculet before any one of us did! And that's a tiny, tiny bird!'

'And I had three lifers!' Siddharth added, thumping his fist into his palm. He glanced at Shoma who was sprawled in a chair nearby, her nose in a book.

'Shoma! Don't tell me you've been slouched in that chair all afternoon and evening,' Meatloaf said loudly with mock horror. 'You really should have come with us! It was so beautiful.'

'I've been fine,' Shoma said, glancing up. 'Sometimes in the forest after the rain, there are terrible insects that bite you right through your clothes ...' She nodded knowingly.

'I got bitten on my neck!' Aditi said. 'Are they poisonous?' She felt her neck tenderly and looked a little alarmed.

'Well if you die in a week, shivering and retching and in excruciating pain and gasping for air, you'll know they're poisonous,' Shoma said with some relish. 'Usually, they prefer biting you on your bottom, especially if you have a big one …'

Meatloaf glanced at her sharply but she radiated innocence.

'At least that's what people say!'

'Aditi, Kalpana – I think you'd better put some disinfectant on your bites,' Vinita Aunty said, 'Some of us did get bitten.'

'That's why I never go into the forest after it rains,' Shoma said virtuously. 'You'd better check yourself for leeches too before they crawl inside you! They can go quite far up your nose and lay their eggs in your brain. And you're in big trouble if they wriggle up your bottom!'

'Shoma!'

She glanced at Brijesh, but he was just looking impassively at Big Djinn.

They were just finishing off with tea in the verandah when Djinn raised his head and growled. Then he got up and went to the top of the steps, staring out at the lake, growling steadily.

'What's the matter, boy?' Shoma went up to him and held him by the collar. If there was another leopard around, she didn't want him rushing off to attack it. She looked at the lake.

'Oh,' she said surprised, 'Nani, someone's coming this way in a very fancy boat from the resort.'

A sleek blue and white speedboat was surging through the lake towards the shore adjoining the flower meadow beneath the garden. Shoma picked up Vinita Aunty's Leica binoculars lying on the table nearby and peered through them.

'It looks like that rich Makhi fellow with his bodyguards and all,' she announced.

Sohan Uncle had got up. 'You mean Shri Suraj Mukhiji himself?' he said with reverence in his voice. 'Shoma dear, let me see!'

'Welcome, welcome Suraj-ji!' Sohan Uncle exclaimed enthusiastically as he greeted the party of three men at the bottom of the steps a few minutes later. They had tied up their speedboat and made their way over.

'So wonderful to see you, ji! You look very well!' Sohan Uncle gushed, embracing his friend. 'Mummy told me about this wonderful project of yours! So amazing – a golf course on top of the mountain. Come in, come in!'

'Ah, you look well too, Sohanji. I think London suits you!' the billionaire builder replied, smiling.

'Come in, ji, and meet my family!' Sohan Uncle said, guiding his friend into the verandah. The two bodyguards followed closely, warily eyeing Djinn, who was being held by Shoma and still growling steadily, his hair standing on end.

'*Kutta baandho!* Tie the dog!' one of them snapped at Shoma, who was appalled by his cheek.

'Kya – what?' she asked incredulously. She looked at Djinn, who really was fizzing away furiously like a volcano about to erupt. 'What's the matter, boy?'

Djinn just stared implacably at the guests and growled on.

'Come on, boy, let's go to the meadow for a walk,' Shoma said, realizing that Djinn was not about to cool down as long as these people were here. She led him down the steps and clipped on his lead, glancing back at the verandah and wondering whether she should call Brijesh. But then she saw Aditi take Brijesh's arm and lead him inside the house after the others. She stuck out her tongue at them and took Djinn out into the meadow.

In the drawing room, the adults had settled down as Kusum brought out tea and fruit cake and samosas for the guests. Shri Suraj Mukhi leaned forward and clasped his hands together.

'Sohanji, perhaps you can be of help to me!' he said and laughed.

Sohan Uncle shook his head. 'Your wish is my command!' he said. 'How can I be of service?' He was flattered – here was one of the country's richest men, a close friend of the Prime Minister no less, asking for his assistance!

'Hanji, well you see, I made your mother-in-law an offer—a very generous offer, I must say—but she has so far declined to accept it ...'

Nani put on what Shoma would have called her 'stubborn' expression.

'And what offer was that?' Sohan Uncle inquired as Vinita Aunty smiled with all her teeth and Professor Damodar and Meatloaf waited agog.

'I want to build a sister resort here!' Shri Suraj Mukhi said. 'Of course, madamji will be given a separate, very spacious villa with all the mod cons as well as a generous settlement ...' He mentioned a figure and Sohan Uncle and Vinita Aunty's eyes popped.

Nani cleared her throat. 'Shri Mukhiji, I explained to you last time that this is our ancestral home and will remain so ...'

Shri Mukhiji went on as if Nani had not spoken. 'You see, I want this place to develop as a sports hub: Sailing, speed-boating, paragliding, fishing, skiing, hiking, trekking, mountain climbing, a water-park for children ... I want to link this place with the golf resort by cable car over the lake. If permission is forthcoming, I want to introduce seaplanes here too!' Shri Mukhiji looked earnest. 'This place is so backward – it must devlope! You realize how much employment these projects will generate? It will completely transform the economy here! Eventually I want to devlope the entire lake waterfront all around! To build villas and condominiums, so people can enjoy life in the lap of nature.'

Sohan Uncle looked gob-smacked and turned to Nani.

'Mummy, you never told us! But did you even consider the offer?' he asked, then added with a smile, 'you could be living in the middle of the Indian equivalent of Davos or some exclusive Swiss resort!'

Shri Suraj Mukhi got to his feet, followed by his bodyguards.

'Achchaji, I'll be going now,' he said, 'Madamji can consider the offer again.' He smiled at Sohan Uncle. 'I hope you have better luck than I did in persuading her!'

Sohan Uncle nodded. 'Well, I will certainly try!' he said, shaking the great man's hand vigorously. 'You have made a very generous offer!'

Shri Suraj Mukhi looked around.

'Where's the little girlie with the big dog?' he asked, inclining his head at Nani. 'Your granddaughter, ji?'

Nani stiffened. 'She's taken the dog to the meadow. Why?'

Suraj Mukhi laughed. 'Ah yes, I see her. So sweet, no? Such a little girl handling such a ferocious, big dog!' He clicked his tongue. 'She is happy living here?'

'Very!' Nani almost snapped. The man was really getting on her nerves.

'Imagine how happy she would be if there were all those sports and a water-park and all! Think about it! Children these days love things like that! There will be plenty of children for her to play with too.'

'She is perfectly happy, thank you! She rides her bicycle, sails her boat, climbs and runs around with her dog …'

'Yes, of course, but in this kind of wild terrain it can be dangerous for a small child. She could fall, or be attacked by a leopard or bear. That must worry you!'

Nani's cheeks began to get red. She rarely got angry but now she was.

'Shoma has Big Djinn with her, and she's just fine,' she said coldly. 'She knows her way around very well.'

'Of course, of course! Achcha, I'll take your leave now, ji! Thank you!'

From the far side of the meadow, Shoma and Djinn watched the guests depart in their boat. Then they made their way back to the house. Only Nani was still in the verandah. It was pretty dark now and the moths had started their dizzy dance around the lights. Nani was gazing out at the lake. She looked up as Shoma came up the stone steps.

'Shoma, sweetie, tell the others to collect their equipment. They've left it all lying on the table.'

'Okay, Nani!' Shoma glanced casually at the gleaming equipment. Really, the Vermas were so careless, leaving such valuable stuff just lying around like this. A small silver MP3 recorder caught her eye. She knew Siddharth used it as a backup just in case his main recorder failed. Her eyes widened. It seemed to be on: the light next to the 'record' button gleamed green. She grinned, switched it off and quietly slipped it into her pocket. Then she went up to call the others.

They were all in her room. Aditi was flashing cards of bird pictures at Brijesh—who looked trapped—and asking him to identify them. Siddharth was talking earnestly (and, he thought, meaningfully) with Kalpana and Arvind was busy playing with his phone.

'Nani wants you to collect your stuff from the verandah!' Shoma announced and then banged the door shut.

Later that evening, after everyone had bathed and changed and gathered in the drawing room, munching salted almonds over their drinks, an awful feeling of alienation swept over Shoma. All the others did—including the traitor Brijesh—was talk about birds; or about binoculars and scopes and cameras and how they had got fabulous bargains on the internet. Come what may, she would not be drawn into the subject. After all, none of them had seemed in the least bit interested in the things *she* was interested in: mountain bikes, boats, pup tents, sketching and painting and rock climbing. Worse, it seemed like the clique of four (plus one?) kids was hatching something. They kept giving her sidelong glances and then looked at one another, winking and nodding conspiratorially.

'So where should we go tomorrow morning?' Professor Damodar asked, looking around.

'The forests on the north side of the lake are interesting,' said Sohan Uncle. 'There are some nice patches where you can come across mixed hunting parties. It's a very good birding area.'

'Those islands at the eastern end look interesting too. Let's go there, okay?' said Meatloaf as if the matter had already been decided. She looked at Nani. 'Aunty, are there any boats one can hire from the town?'

'Oh, Shoma has a boat, didn't she tell you?'

'Nani, please!'

'Shoma has a *boat*?' Siddharth sounded incredulous and in spite of the fact that Nani had let out the equivalent of a state secret, Shoma couldn't help gloating over the pure envy in his voice.

'Yes,' Nani went on mildly, unaware of what she had done. 'She goes all over the lake in it. It even has a little engine, doesn't it, Budgie? Her father gave it to her as a birthday gift. Of course, she wears a life jacket at all times and lets us know when she's going ...'

'Oh, that's great, no problem then! Shoma will be able to take us to the islands tomorrow!' Meatloaf decided, as if *Rubadubdub* was hers.

'It's too small,' Shoma said. Good grief, if Meatloaf sat in *Rubadubdub* it would sink like a stone, poor thing.

'If it has an outboard motor it won't matter – you could make trips up and down ...'

'Or Professor Damodar or Sohan Uncle could skipper it. You needn't come at all if you want to read comics or something instead.'

'Nani, how can they all go? They don't have life jackets,' Shoma pointed out. 'You made me promise to wear mine all the time!'

'Umm ... maybe with Sohan Uncle and Damodar Uncle around, it'll be okay.'

'The lake can be very dangerous,' Shoma said darkly. 'The waves can get big very quickly.'

'But ... but where is the boat?' Siddharth asked, puzzled. 'We've been here six days and haven't seen it.'

'Yes, where is this great boat?' Aditi asked. 'And why didn't you show it to us?'

'Because it's a private boat, that's why!'

'Well, you'll have to show it to us tomorrow.'

'So good then, that's settled!' Meatloaf said. 'How many people can your boat take?'

'Depends on the size of the people,' Shoma replied pointedly.

'Okay, then with average people?' Meatloaf smiled as if she were talking to someone very slow-witted.

'Four: one up front, one at the back and two in the middle.'

'Good, we'll sort out the trips tomorrow morning. But let's aim to leave by 6 a.m., okay?'

'Great!'

'Shoma, if you'll tell us where the boat is moored we'll manage ourselves. No need for you to get up early and all that, my dear.'

A hot flame of anger burned inside Shoma; now they were trying to hijack *Rubadubdub* from right under her nose. The cheek! She'd be damned if she let them take it out. Again, the conversation had veered off to birds, and Shoma tuned out. The wheels in her sharp brain were whirring …

'Nani, I'm just fetching a book from my room,' she said just before getting into bed, after having tucked Djinn into his own bed in the verandah that night.

Actually, she had just wanted to check out her room to make sure the other kids hadn't been messing around with her things. Besides, she had realized that she had left behind one especially precious sketch-pad that had a series of paintings of the lake. She paused outside the door, her ear pressed to it. Oh, yes, they were all there – she could hear Siddharth's hateful voice and all the others laughing at something clever he had just said. They were having a good time, no doubt about that. She raised her hand to knock. But then again, it was her room, so why the hell did she have to knock? She shoved the door handle down and barged in. All five of them were sitting on her bed, playing Uno with her pack of cards. They giggled as she entered. Brijesh looked at her, almost apologetically, but she could see he was being held prisoner by Aditi who kept staring at him with wide eyes. Also on the bed were a plate of chocolate biscuits and a big plastic bottle of Coke.

'Hi. You want something?' Aditi inquired, raising her eyebrows and nudging Brijesh as Bony Mouse stifled a giggle.

'Umm ... Brijesh, Nani wants to talk to you,' she fibbed. 'She asked me to fetch you!' Brijesh got off the bed and joined her at the door.

'Don't worry, there are no birds here!' Siddharth said, looking around the room, and then frowned. 'Actually, I did think I heard a forest owlet outside the window, though ... you might want to close your ears before it calls again ...'

A ripple of laughter went through the bunch.

'Wait here!' Shoma ordered Brijesh like she was giving Djinn a command. She walked over to her bedside table and retrieved her precious sketch-book.

'It's so nice of you to let us use your boat,' Siddharth said, 'even if you didn't tell us about it all this time.'

'Say, Siddharth, how many bird calls have you recorded?' Zit-face asked, lying back on the bed and making poor

Shoma wince. She'd have to clean the head-rest thoroughly once these creeps left; the fellow had oily hair.

'Fifty-six, including the ones I made today,' Siddharth said. 'And you know the best part? For most of them, papa took videos too. So they are perfect for identification purposes. Would you like to see them again?'

'Hey, Aditi, pass me some of those chocolate biscuits, please!' Zit-face said.

Oh no! They were *eating* on her bed! They'd scatter crumbs all over her bed and make a mess. And chocolate biscuits – there'd be ants everywhere in no time! Shoma leaned forward and snatched at the plate of biscuits from Aditi. Aditi dodged her and disgorged all the biscuits onto the bed.

'Now look what you've done!' Shoma yelled. 'I have one rule in my room. No one eats on the bed! Pick them up and brush the crumbs away right now!'

'My, my, what a prima donna!' Siddharth spoke in that mincing way that made her gnash her teeth. 'She's ordering us around again!' He picked up a biscuit and bit into it messily, deliberately scattering crumbs and small pieces everywhere.

'You should just see her,' Aditi said spitefully, 'She spends the whole day in those disgusting overalls, splashing mud all over them, and now tells us not to eat on the bed! Just the other day she turned up covered with mud and slime from head to toe!'

'Shoma,' said Zit-face earnestly, and suddenly Shoma became aware that he was staring at her in a disconcerting sort of way. 'You know I just can't believe it. I mean you live in this beautiful place and haven't become interested in birds!'

'Don't try to convert her,' Siddharth grinned. 'It won't work. We've tried all our lives and gotten nowhere. She's stubborn as a mule.'

Aditi was shaking her head slowly at Bony Mouse and murmuring, 'Not her fault really, poor thing. Her parents are divorcing and just dumped her here. They don't give a shit about her, and poor Nani has to do everything, mama says ...'

'Don't you bring my parents into this, you slimy witch!' Shoma shouted, but she was angry not so much at Aditi's words but because she could feel the sudden tears pricking — and because Brijesh was still watching her from the doorway.

'Well it's true! If they cared a tuppence about you they wouldn't have dumped you here in the back of beyond. And it's no wonder.' Aditi raised her eyebrows and drew in a deep breath. 'You know,' she said piously, 'in most cases when parents divorce, they fight each other over who's to get custody of the children. In Shoma's case, they're probably fighting because neither of them wants her!' She turned to Shoma. 'Dumped you, dumped you, your parents dumped you!'

'That's not true! Take it back!' Shoma screeched. 'I'll teach you such a lesson!'

'You will? Hah! Let's see!' Suddenly, Aditi leaned forward and snatched the sketch-book out of Shoma's hands. 'Ah, and what do we have here?' she smirked, flipping through the pages.

'Give it back!'

'Try and get it!' Aditi dodged. 'My God,' she said, 'what a load of horrors! And Nani thinks you paint well!'

'Give it back, give it back, you bitch!' Shoma leapt at her but Aditi backed away, grinning. Swiftly, she placed the book open-faced on the bedside table. 'There you are! But first I'll improve the paintings.' And very deliberately she poured half the contents of the Coke bottle over the pad. 'There, now they look so much better, don't you think?'

'You, you … you!' Shoma screamed. 'My paintings! I'll kill you! I'll kill you!' She flung herself on Aditi and whacked her twice tightly across the face. Then she pushed her back on to the bed and pinned her down, kneeling over her and pummelling her with her fists and yanking her hair, screaming, 'Take it back, take it back!' The others looked aghast. Siddharth tried pulling her back, and got a tooth-rattling punch in the jaw for his trouble.

'I hate you all!' Shoma screamed, 'get out of my room!' She lunged again at Aditi who was trying to fend her off, screeching.

'Kalpana, quick, call Nani and papa – tell them Shoma's gone ballistic,' Siddharth squawked as Bony Mouse vacated the bed with alacrity and fled, white-faced, past a stunned Brijesh.

'I think, before anything else, Shoma must apologize!' Meatloaf declared, her arms folded across her big bosom. She had taken control of the situation, as poor Nani dithered, not quite knowing how to tackle the crisis. 'I mean, you can't go around attacking people like that!'

Siddharth shook his head slowly. 'She just leapt on Aditi like a slavering wolverine,' he said, feeling his jaw, 'attacked her as if she had rabies.'

'Absolutely!' Vinita Aunty agreed, her face tight with anger, a protective arm around Aditi, who was sniffing and choking back sobs. Shoma had whacked her solidly – the marks of her fingers were clear on Aditi's pale cheeks and one eye was beginning to blacken. 'Poor baby, now go and put some Betadine and ice on that in case she's scratched you. God knows her nails must be septic. Maybe we could show it to the doctor tomorrow and get you a tetanus shot.'

'Yes, Shoma dear, I think you better apologize. You can't treat your guests in that way!' Nani was hugely distressed. Had she brought up her displaced little Budgie all wrong, she wondered. She was at such a difficult age and stage now … between being a rebellious teenager and a lovely young lady. Nani was quite close to tears herself, which made poor Shoma even more upset.

'Nani, do you know what that witch said?' Shoma said, swallowing a sob that was rising dangerously and jabbing a finger at Aditi. 'And then she purposely spilled Coke all over my paintings …'

'Shoma! Mind what you say!' Sohan Uncle snapped. 'We've had about enough of your backchat!'

'Not enough,' Shoma shot back, 'that's what I think!'

'Shoma! Apologize!'

'Will not! I have nothing to apologize for!'

'Go to your room at once!' Vinita Aunty and Sohan Uncle snapped together.

'I *am* in my own room. Why don't you all go to yours and leave me in peace?'

'Shoma!'

'Such cheek! There's no hope for that girl!'

'Bad genes, what else and complete parental neglect!'

The gang of four was looking completely shell-shocked. Such backtalk! Brijesh had a curious expression on his face, a mixture of shock and awe. But it was all becoming a little too much for him too. Quietly, he slunk off into his own room, leaving the door open. He opened a big flat wooden box, lifted out a beautiful almost-finished model of a olive-green Lancaster bomber and quietly began working on it. Meanwhile, in Shoma's room, the matter was beginning to reach boiling point.

'Shall we all just go to bed and deal with this in the morning?' Nani suggested tearfully. She hated such situations.

'No, I think we need to get this over with right now, ma!' Vinita Aunty snapped. 'You're always putting things off and letting them slide. Shoma needs to be disciplined right now.'

'What do you mean?'

'She needs to know she cannot get away with such behaviour!'

'Do you know what that witch told me?' Shoma said, jabbing a finger towards Aditi again. 'Will you even listen?'

'Shoma, we've heard and seen enough.'

'You haven't! She purposely spoiled my paintings.' She was angry again, because the tears were not too far away and she didn't want to cry in front of this lot.

But Nani had spotted the ruined sketch-book and went up to it.

'How did this happen?' she asked, holding it up and shaking her head sorrowfully.

'Nani, the Coke bottle fell on it when Shoma pounced on me,' Aditi said glibly, and the others nodded.

'You bloody liar,' Shoma shouted, appalled. They had all ganged up against her. And that booby Brijesh, who could have vouched for her, had run away to his room! She turned her guns on them again: 'You … you liars … All of you!'

'That's enough. This is something your parents ought to have done long ago!' Vinita Aunty strode over to her table and picked up Shoma's very own broad, eighteen-inch wooden ruler.

'Bend over!' she snapped.

The gang of four snickered. This was going to be good.

'What?' Shoma said uncomprehendingly and Nani gasped.

'Vinita … dear …'

'Ma – keep out of this. I know what I'm doing.'

Meatloaf nodded approvingly.

'I said bend over, Shoma.'

'Why?' Shoma eyed the ruler warily. Vinita Aunty was smacking it smartly against her palm.

'Because you need to be disciplined. Now bend over!'

'I won't and you can't make me!'

Moving more swiftly than Shoma would have believed possible, Vinita Aunty strode over to her and whacked her stingingly on her bottom with the ruler. It made a noise like a pistol shot and the gang of four burst into shocked giggles.

'This'll teach you to attack my Aditi,' Vinita Aunty snapped, raising the ruler again.

Shoma gasped, and then just stood still, transfixed by shock.

'You will not attack or swear at anyone again in this house! Is that clear?' Vinita Aunty said slowly, and brought down the ruler stingingly again. Meatloaf nodded righteously, looking as if she would have liked to have spanked Shoma herself.

'Owwch!'

'Vinita, that's enough! Stop it!'

The gang of four was laughing openly now, even Aditi. In his room, Brijesh stood stock still.

Phatak! The ruler came whistling down again, catching Shoma on her calves.

Brijesh came out into the corridor, his heart beating fast: someone was getting a nasty hiding!

Shoma gave a choked gulp and fled from the room. She ran straight into Brijesh, standing tentatively in the corridor in his pajamas, almost trembling with nervousness. He hated violence of any kind. Shoma cannoned into him, sending him staggering back, her arms instinctively clutching him around the waist. A gigantic sob erupted from her as if her heart had just broken into many, many pieces. Instinctively, he clutched her back, and for a long moment they just held on to each other tightly, saying nothing. For a fleeting second, Shoma got the distinct feeling that he was deliberately hugging her close. Was he trying to comfort her? Not possible! She fled to Nani's room, leaving a hiccupping trail of sobs in her wake. When Nani walked wearily to her room fifteen minutes later, Shoma seemed to be fast asleep in her bed, lying on her stomach with her face buried in her pillow. If Nani had looked closely, she would have noticed that the pillow was dark with tears. And if her hearing had been as good as it once was she might have heard the muffled sobs, burying deep into the pillow.

But Nani had taken her glasses off and saw and heard nothing. She did, however, lean over and gently kiss the back of her Budgie's head before she took a sleeping pill and got ready for bed.

4

It was still pitch dark when Shoma awoke. She glanced at the luminous hands of the bedside clock: it was only 4.45 a.m. Next to her, Nani snored gently. She slunk out of bed and went to the bathroom. As the events of the previous night washed over her again, a lump arose in her throat and she swallowed it angrily and glared at her reflection in the mirror.

'Stop snivelling!' she snapped. 'Stop being such a wuss!' But the sheer injustice of what had happened, festered like a venomous barb embedded in her. What hurt most of all, was what Aditi had said and done and how the others had lied to protect her, and the utter humiliation of being spanked with that ruler in front of everyone, especially Brijesh, who was an outsider. She brushed away a sudden tear and sniffed.

'So what are you going to do about it?' she asked herself. What could she do? The enemy was formidable and stood united, unwilling even to listen to her point of view. Even if they did hear her out, they wouldn't believe her. She brushed her teeth and changed into a sleeveless T-shirt, shorts and denim overalls, nodding slowly as she planned. One thing she was certain about: she was not taking that hideous lot anywhere in *Rubadubdub*. She didn't care how much trouble she would get into. This meant that neither she nor *Rubadubdub* ought to be anywhere close to the house for the whole day. She nodded. Okay, now she had a plan.

She tiptoed to the kitchen and opened the fridge. The Vermas had brought a huge stock of energy bars, chocolate and cheese – as if you couldn't get anything to eat in the whole of India. Shoma swept a generous amount into her backpack and then filled her battered stainless steel flask with water and picked up some apples and pears and half a loaf of bread. Right, that would do, at least for the day. Maybe she could catch some fish on the lake and fry it up too. There was a small battered saucepan and bottle of olive oil, a couple of limes and a twist of salt and pepper stored in the boat just for this. There were also two tins, one wriggling with juicy earthworms and the other stuffed with fat beetle larvae, which she used as fish bait.

Shoma added a packet of dog food for Djinn and padded off to the 'godown', where she put her sketch-pads and pencils and paints into the backpack. In her best handwriting, which really was quite good, she wrote a brief note:

> Dear Nani,
> I've taken 'Rubadubdub' and Big Djinn out for the day. Be back in the evening before dark, I promise. Don't worry. Love and xxxx,
> Budgie

She stuck the note on Nani's dressing table mirror and hoisted her backpack on her slender shoulders. In the drawing room, the curtains were drawn across the big verandah doors, but there was a light on outside as usual – that was where Djinn slept, after all. But the curtains seemed not to have been drawn properly and were swinging slightly back and forth. Surely there wasn't anyone out there! She tiptoed to the door and parted the curtains, noticing at once that the sliding doors were open. There *was* someone out there! She peered into the verandah.

It was just like yesterday: Brijesh, rocking back and forth in the rocking chair, staring at the faintly glimmering waters of the lake, with Djinn watchfully curled up on his bed nearby. Djinn raised his head immediately on noticing her and thumped his tail. Quietly, she drew back the door and stepped into the verandah, even as Brijesh whirled around almost guiltily and Djinn came up to her and licked her hand, wagging his tail.

'He let you come out?' she asked, surprised. 'He didn't growl at you or anything?'

'Oh ... hello, no ... he just thumped his tail and watched me!' His face lit up with a wry grin. 'I made no sudden moves!'

'Oh!' She swallowed. 'I guess he must like you!' If Djinn liked him, he couldn't be too bad, she thought.

'You're going out at this hour?' he asked. He was still in his pajamas and a sleeveless pullover and his hair was all rumpled.

'Um, yes!' She gulped. 'Would you like to come along? I'm going out for the whole day. I'm taking Djinn, of course!' It was not so much that she wanted his company as it was to get him away from that clingy Aditi. It would be one royally up her snooty nose if she could hijack Brijesh for the whole day!

'Oh, okay, sure, I don't mind!' he got up. 'I'll just change in a jiffy.'

'Roll the doors back quietly – they rumble!' she warned.

'Um … where are you planning to go?' he asked as he joined her shortly afterwards. He was in jeans, a yellow T-shirt, and a dark blue pullover and hiking boots.

'We'll take *Rubadubdub* out to one of the islands at the eastern end of the lake,' she replied.

'They won't mind?' he said, vaguely indicating the house, as they went down the steps to the garden.

'They can go to hell!'

'Oh, ya, sure, I guess …'

'Don't worry, I've got stuff to eat!' She grinned. 'I stole some of their energy bars and chocolate and cheese, and we'll catch some fish!' She eyed him curiously. 'Um … why were you sitting there, all by yourself?'

He shrugged. 'I couldn't sleep. And it's very nice and cool outside.' He glanced at Djinn, trotting by their side, waving his tail happily.

She took him to the spot where *Rubadubdub* lay moored, covered with brushwood and fallen pine branches.

'Papa gave this to me for my birthday,' she said proudly as they cleared the branches away. 'I had to hide her from the others.' She took the military green tarpaulin cover off the gleaming white outboard motor and folded it away.

Djinn jumped in and sat at the prow. Shoma frowned.

'Can you row?' she asked.

He shrugged. 'I haven't done it before …'

'We'll have to row at first. I don't want to start the engine here – the noise might wake up someone at the house. Okay, you sit near the engine: I'll row!'

She strapped on her Day-Glo orange life jacket, pulled out a pair of bright orange and purple oars from the bottom of the boat and sat down in the middle. Tentatively, Brijesh sat down beside the spanking white outboard. Shoma pushed an oar against the shore, and then dug both oars into the water as they swung out into the lake.

'Here we go!'

There was a gauzy blue-grey mist over the water and the faintest flush of orange towards the east. The only sound was the faint clop and plash of the oars as they dug into the water. Shoma rowed steadily for a while, her face puckering up with the effort, her tongue peeking out between her lips. Brijesh watched her quietly. They slipped out of sight of the house and she shipped the oars.

'Okay, we can use the outboard now,' she said. 'You come over here and I'll start her up.'

They exchanged places carefully. She settled beside the outboard and lowered it into the water along with the tiller. 'Here we go!' She yanked the cord and the motor gurgled and then roared into muffled life. The boat surged forwards.

'Watch what I do, and I'll let you drive on the way back,' she offered. He nodded.

There were three islands dotting the eastern shore arranged in a 'U'. Shoma steered towards the one in the middle, furthest from the shoreline.

'There's a small cove where we'll land,' she explained, 'with a tiny beach that faces the lake so no one on the shore will be able to see the boat.'

As they approached, the island loomed ahead. As she had said, it was thickly forested and steep-sloped. It was a marvel how the pines and deodars and ferns clung on and grew out of the almost vertical rock faces.

'We can climb right to the top,' Shoma said, watching Brijesh. 'But first we'll try and catch some fish in the cove.' She switched off the engine and took up the oars again. 'We have to be careful as we get in,' she explained, 'There are rocks jutting out all over.' Deftly, she maneuvered the boat between moss-covered rocks.

'You're good!' he said and she flushed with pleasure.

'There's a fishing rod in that long box beneath your seat,' she said. 'Take it out.'

It was a neat fiberglass rod in two sections with a reel and fishing line attached to it. Shoma shipped the oars and took the rod from Brijesh. They drifted silently, watching the half-frozen, dew-pearled dragonflies, perched on the stalks, waiting for the sun.

'What are you going to use as bait?' he asked.

She grinned and took out a pair of battered tins from the bottom of the boat, both with tiny holes on the top.

'I've got earthworms in mud in one and beetle grubs in wood shavings in the other,' she said, handing them over. 'We'll use the beetle grubs. Take one out and put it on the hook!'

'Um, sure!'

Djinn watched interestedly as Brijesh dug around in the box and eventually pulled out an enormous white beetle larva. 'Wow, it's like a barrage balloon!' he said.

'Okay, hook it!' Shoma said brutally, 'but be careful — it may bite!'

She took the rod from him and cast the line into the water.

'Now we wait for a bite. I hope the fish are as hungry as I am!'

'Um … normally you do this sort of thing on your own?' he asked. She nodded.

'Ya … well, there's no one else around. But I have Djinn. And now you've come along! By the way, thanks for not squealing about yesterday … you know, the pea-shooter thing …' Suddenly she stared sharply at him. 'You didn't, did you?'

He shook his head, a little grin lighting up his face. 'No! Your aim is very good! You got all four of them!'

'They deserved it!'

They sat in companionable silence for a while. It was tranquil. The eastern sky had begun to flush orange and the mists moved around gently over the water. The dragonflies, still dewy, looked like they had been gilded. They occasionally beat their wings experimentally to heat up their mighty flight muscles but didn't dare to take off from the stalks they were perched on just yet. Brijesh sat back. It was so peaceful here; his mom would have loved it. He gulped.

Shoma looked at the fishing rod. 'I wish we'd get a bite!' She'd barely finished saying that when the rod jerked violently in her hands and dipped right into the water. 'I got a bite!' she squealed. Something enormous and silver thrashed out of the lake and plunged back in. Shoma gripped the rod with both hands and began reeling in. 'He's very strong and heavy,' she squawked, 'I don't think I can hold him or bring him in!' She braced her feet against the side of the boat. The rod bent alarmingly, but the fishing line held firm. The monster on the hook thrashed wildly.

Brijesh paused for a moment. He could see she was rapidly losing the battle with the fish: she just didn't have the sheer physical strength to haul it in on her own. He knew he could take the rod from her and bring it in. But it was *her* catch and she had to bring it in even if with a little help. Swiftly, he slipped over and got behind her. He put his arms around her waist and took hold of the rod along with her.

'Okay, steady now,' he grunted straight into her shell-pink ear. 'We'll have it! Push the butt of the rod against your tummy and reel him! Whew, he's strong!' They held on for dear life as the fish fought and twisted. Suddenly, Shoma felt her little heart thump, flutter and thud. She had never been held so close by a boy in her entire life: well, last night perhaps, but that had been for just an instant; but now he was literally holding on to her tightly as if he never wanted to let her go!

They held on for several minutes, not letting the rod dip beneath the surface of the water, as the fish thrashed and struggled and the rod bent alarmingly.

'He's a fighter!' Brijesh muttered, helping her reel it back. 'A real heavyweight! But we'll have him!'

'Uh-huh!' Shoma squeaked.

'Okay, let's bring him up now,' he grunted after a few minutes and yanked up the rod. 'I think he's tiring!'

They jerked the rod upwards and towards the boat and suddenly there was the fish, flapping about wildly in the bottom of the boat, still not giving up. It was about two feet long, heavy and still fighting mad, thumping about at the bottom of the boat.

'Get it!' Shoma squealed as Djinn barked encouragement.

Brijesh grabbed it, thrashing frantically, the hook still in its gaping mouth, and clutched it to his chest.

'He's heavy!' he said, 'must be at least three kilos. Hang on to the rod!' He took ahold of its head in a chokehold.

'Keep still!'

The fish gasped, opening its fearsome mouth even wider, its gills opening and closing frantically.

'Okay!' he told Shoma, 'I've got him good. Now take the hook out of his mouth!'

She nodded, 'Okay!'

'Quickly, I can't hold him still for very long – he's strong and slippery!' She came forward and deftly removed the barbed hook from the gaping mouth. Brijesh looked at her.

'I think we'll let him go now!' he gulped, 'He's a fighter and deserves to win! We'll catch another one.'

Her eyes were round and big as grapefruit as she watched him release the fish back into the lake. Dumbly, she nodded. Brijesh's eyes had welled up suddenly and angrily he wiped the tears away.

'Why … what's the matter?'

He stared at her, his defenses suddenly down. 'You know, mom was a fighter too … right to the very end!' he said brokenly, 'She deserved to win. But she didn't! It sucks!'

'Oh,' she whispered. 'I'm so sorry!' The little boat wobbled as she got up and put her arms around him and hugged him tightly, her face buried in his shoulder. She didn't know what else to do. He clutched her back, not quite sure whether it was because the boat had begun rocking or he simply needed to hug someone. She looked up into his surprised face, a small smile breaking out.

'You're as good as God, if not better!' she said fiercely, her arms still around him, 'He didn't save your mom but you saved the fish in spite of it being our breakfast!' Her eyes flashed mischievously. 'But now what are we going to eat for breakfast?'

'We'll catch another one,' he said. 'Let's put another worm on the hook!'

To their delight, they did catch another fish about fifteen minutes later: smaller than the previous one, but nicely plump and not a feisty fighter at all.

'Okay, let's get ashore and fry this up,' Shoma said. 'I'm starving!'

The little shingle beach was beautiful, surrounded by the pine and deodar forests that seemed to climb down the mountain.

'We'll make a fire now,' Shoma said. 'Collect all those pine needles and pine cones and dry twigs, and scrape off some of the resin from the trees. You know, it's like turpentine and catches fire easily! Be careful, it's very sticky.'

'How are we going to light the fire?' he asked.

'We'll have to rub two sticks together like they did in cave-men times,' she said, her eyes sparkling.

'Oh!'

'Or we can use this,' she said, producing a small pink plastic cigarette lighter from the boat. 'I always carry this in the boat.'

'What about all the cheese and chocolate and energy bars?'

'We'll be hungry again very soon – we'll have them then. Besides, we're going to climb up to the top of the island after breakfast.'

Expertly, she gutted and filleted the fish and put it in the saucepan with olive oil, where it sizzled aromatically. She squeezed some lime juice over it and sprinkled some salt and pepper. They took turns spiking pieces on her penknife and eating them.

'Careful of the bones,' she said.

'It's very good!' he said, 'And you've stashed an entire kitchen in your boat!' Big Djinn had settled down beside them, wolfing down his dog food, which she emptied onto a convenient flat rock.

'Okay, now we go up!'

He glanced up at the forested mountain towering right above them. The slope seemed almost vertical and he couldn't figure out how the heck they were going to climb up.

'We just climb up that cliff? What about Djinn?'

She grinned. 'Actually, there's a secret route that I discovered,' she said. 'Follow me now!'

She led him to the edge of the beach, where a stream tinkled out of a crack in the cliff face. 'Be careful, the rocks can be slippery. We just climb up alongside it. If you notice, the rocks are nicely arranged like steps. There's a lovely pool about halfway up with a waterfall at one end, where I paddle. We cross over to the other side of the pool and then continue up to the top alongside the waterfall!'

'Oh, wow! You found this on your own?'

'Well, actually Djinn did! So I call it Djinn's Stairway to Heaven!' She smiled at him, and held out her hand. 'Come along now!'

The pool was lovely – a deep sapphire blue with silver ripples, shimmering with gauzy-winged dragonflies.

'Is it deep?' he asked.

She nodded. 'It's shallow on this side and deep on that end, where the waterfall is. I've only paddled in the shallow part.' She smiled at him again. 'Maybe you can teach me how to swim properly here!'

'Okay! Sure!'

They waded across; it was about knee deep. Djinn splashed through happily. The climb thereon was steep but not difficult. At last, they emerged at the top. The view was stupendous, only spoilt by the hideous new resort and the flattened mountaintop golf course at its distant western end. There was another small island which Brijesh hadn't noticed so far, perhaps a hundred metres offshore from the eastern edge of the golf course. Below them lay the lake, deep blue and emerald green, sparkling in the sun. A cool breeze fanned their faces. They sat down side by side on a smooth flat grassy knoll, their backs against a rock.

'Do you like Aditi?' Shoma asked suddenly. 'She was all over you yesterday.'

He looked a little uncomfortable. 'Yeah, I know … she was a bit too touchy-feely!'

'But do you like her?'

'She's okay, I guess. I hardly know her, but …'

'But? But what?'

He smiled suddenly, and she thought he really looked cute when he did, because two front teeth peeped out as if they were smiling too. 'Um … she's not as nice as someone who thinks I'm better than God!'

She flushed red. 'What ... what was your mom like?' she blurted before she could stop herself. 'Sorry!' she gulped but it was too late. 'I shouldn't have asked that!'

He swallowed. 'Mom was great. She was very clever, doing research on and designing rocket engines and satellites and stuff like that. But she also taught me a lot of normal things: how to cook, how to swim, how to do first-aid and how to defend myself. She used to laugh a lot and we went on treks. She got me all my model planes too ... She used to tease me and say, "If you want to be a proper man, you should know how to cook and sew, make flowers grow!" Those were lines from a song by Bob Dylan, one of her favourite singers. In spite of papa, she was always laughing. She kept saying we have to make the best of the hand we've been dealt – no point complaining about it because it's not going to change!'

Shoma's eyes widened. 'You mean your mom knew karate and all that stuff?'

He nodded. 'She was one of those all-rounders.' He shook his head and his face darkened. 'The only mistake she made was to marry papa! She said he was very different when she did. But he was so jealous of her because she was so much better than him at everything!'

Shoma shook her head. 'No, if she hadn't married him you wouldn't be here!' She eyed him again. She just had to ask.

'Um ... yesterday, you know when I jumped on Aditi ...'

'Umm ... I think I'd gone to my room after that. I don't like people fighting and that kind of thing.'

'But ... but then you came out and hugged me when I ran out of the room.'

He smiled wryly but went red too. 'Um ... you sort of ran straight into me and looked like you needed a hug.' And maybe he had also needed to hug someone?

'I only attacked Aditi because she said that mama and papa don't want me to live with them! Do you think that could be true? I've been living with Nani for five years ...'

'What a horrible thing to say!'

'And all the others covered up for her!' She knew she was tattling, but sometimes you just had to. 'So now they think I'm lying. They wouldn't even hear me out!'

'That's not fair!'

Shoma then told Brijesh everything that had happened.

'But do you think it is true?' she went on. 'That mama and papa are fighting over not wanting to keep me? That they dumped me on Nani?'

'No.' He frowned. 'But who would you like to stay with? Suppose they asked you ...'

'I have to choose one?'

'Uh-huh. You could visit the other one every weekend or whatever.'

'Not possible! Papa lives in Bangalore and Mama spends most of her time in Paris. Besides, then Nani will be all alone again.'

'So maybe it's best that you live with your Nani. Do they visit you?'

'Yes, but not very often,' she grinned. 'So then they feel guilty and buy me expensive gifts!'

He grinned, 'Then you're on a good wicket!'

She smiled, 'I guess. I'm going to ask papa for a pup tent and camping and climbing gear now.'

'Good for you!'

He was leaning back against the rock, squinting up at the heavens. It was a brilliantly sunny day, beginning to get hot now. The sky was piercing blue. 'Oh,' he said suddenly. 'Do you have your binoculars?'

'Yes. Why?' She screwed up her face. 'Are *you* bird-watching now?' But she gave them to him.

'There's a raptor up there,' he said, focusing the binoculars, 'flying in tight circles.'

'So?'

'Here, have a look! Right up there …'

'Are you trying to make me a bird-watcher?' she asked, irritated. 'Because I'm not interested.'

A flock of rock pigeons suddenly erupted from one of the rock faces on the adjoining island.

'Oh my God – Shoma, look!'

In spite of herself, she looked up. She spotted the tiny arrowhead-like speck immediately. It was swooping down at an incredible speed even as the pigeon flock whirled around in a circle, right overhead.

'It's … it's like a meteor!' she whispered.

The peregrine whistled down steeply, making a noise like a descending shell, right behind the panic-stricken pigeons. It targeted its victim and slammed into it from behind, not ten yards from the watching children. There was a muffled explosion as the pigeon disintegrated and a cloud of grey feathers wafted down. The bird fell, thumping softly to earth a few yards away from the children. Djinn got to his feet with a half-growl even as the peregrine landed squarely on the bird, dug its talons into its chest and took off again, flapping its wings hard. It flew off to an adjoining island and landed on a small rocky ledge.

'Wow!' Brijesh breathed. 'Did you see that? It might have a nest on that ledge!' He glanced at Shoma.

She was rummaging frantically in her knapsack, taking out her sketch-pad and colours.

'I have to paint that!' she said, 'Right *now*! Or I'll forget!' She glanced at him. 'You can take Djinn for a walk around the island,' she suggested.

To Brijesh's surprise, the big dog got to his feet when he called him and shambled alongside him, sniffing here and there, his bushy curly tail waving jauntily. Brijesh was still a little wary of him and didn't dare pet him just yet. It had become hot; the sun was strong so he removed his pullover.

'You must feel really hot wearing that fur coat all the time!' he told Djinn. They walked all around the island. It was covered with pine trees but had little paths weaving their way in between them. The drops nearly everywhere were sheer.

They returned to Shoma after about an hour, and sat
down quietly a little distance away from her. Quietly, Brijesh
watched her work. She was bent over her sketch-pad, her
watercolours at her side, dipping and dabbing with her
brushes and then sitting back and squinting critically at what
she had done, whistling softly and tunefully as she worked.
Djinn seemed to know the drill too: she was not to be
disturbed. He lay down next to Brijesh and thumped his tail
on the ground, panting happily.

Again, a sense of peace and tranquility overcame Brijesh
and he thought once more of his mother. She had taken him
on treks out of Mumbai, most recently to Tunganeshwar, and
had loved the outdoors. The outdoor adventures had stopped
once she had fallen ill: she'd been drained of all her energy
and vitality by the rapacious disease. And yet she had fought
like mad till the bitter end. He had spent a lot of time in
her hospital room, quietly building the last model she had
bought for him: the Lancaster bomber. She had died before
he had finished it.

Not for a second did he think about his father.

Then he picked up the binoculars and scanned the
surroundings. For a while he focused them on the resort
and golf course at the other end, far away. The mountaintop
was flat and bald, with just a single row of pines bisecting
it, like a mohawk haircut. It seemed like the ridge at the
top had been broadened by rocks and boulders built up
like a supporting wall from the steep slopes. Even so, the
golfers would have a very hard time ensuring their balls

didn't roll over the ridge edge. And then there was that adjacent little island with a smooth green on it too ... No 8, with bunkers on either side. So from the main course, it appeared that the golfers had to hit the ball across the lake and then probably take a boat across and hit it back to the main course! It was quite an obstacle course! Below, on a narrow rocky ledge, were the resort and a villa. (Shri Mukhiji had been inspired by the pictures of dramatic Austrian and German castles perched on similar precarious ledges.) Steps led down to it from the golf course above. It seemed like a crazy location for a resort and villa – and a golf course, for that matter.

'Can I see what you've done?' he asked Shoma a little later as she packed up her things, still whistling. She seemed to have done a series of paintings. There were three parchment sheets laid out, held down by rocks, drying off.

'Okay,' she said, 'I don't mind!'

He came over and looked at the paintings. They were not so much about the bird per se as they were about speed, blurring colours, the sheer violence and power of the kill and the final proud triumph of the hunter.

'Wow!' he said, 'you're really good!'

'Nah – I know they don't really look like the bird herself, but of what she did!' But she was pleased by his praise.

She reached into her backpack and took out the food she had purloined from the fridge. 'Let's eat! This place always makes me hungry.' She bit into an energy bar as he unwrapped a wedge of cheese.

'Wow, this is Camembert! My favourite!' He cut a section and folded it in a hunk of bread. 'You are really going to get into trouble, you know!'

'There's some stinky cheese too,' she said wickedly. 'I think you'll like that!'

He smiled at her. 'You know, they're going to put you in jail! By the way, you whistle very well. You sound just like a bird!'

'I do *not!*'

He was grinning at her, teasing her.

'Um … what did your mom look like?' she asked suddenly. 'Do you have a picture?'

He fished one out of his wallet and handed it over without looking at it.

'Wow! She was so pretty!' The lady in the picture had brown eyes, a friendly laughing mouth, and black hair that curled up from her shoulders. She looked very happy.

'Um … could I keep this, please?' she asked unexpectedly, 'Do you have another?'

'Oh, sure, I guess! But why?'

'Just like that!' she smiled, 'She was such a pretty lady!' She leant back against Djinn. 'I'm feeling sleepy.'

He lay back on the soft cushiony grass too and gazed at the sky. 'You know,' he told her, 'this place would make a very good runway for my Lancaster. She's almost ready. We could fly her from here …'

'Uh-huh!' she murmured as her eyes closed gently and she drifted off to sleep.

They awoke with a start a few hours later, hot, sweaty, sunburned and hungry and thirsty again. They polished off the bread and cheese and chocolate, leaving just the fruit for later.

'I'm so hot!' Shoma complained. Her bright eyes sparkled. 'We should have slept under the pine trees, not out in the open like this. Hey, maybe we should go down to the pool and cool off. You could give me my first swimming lesson!'

'What? But we don't have swimsuits ...'

'Doesn't matter. We'll swim in our clothes! They'll be dry by the time we get home.'

He shrugged. 'Okay!'

But this morning, she had neglected to look at the sky – she had been too engrossed in her painting. The stickiness and faint opalescent haze were back, and far away the mountains rumbled.

They threaded their way back down to the waterfall pool. Brijesh took off his T-shirt and jeans – he had black running shorts on underneath. Shoma stripped to her T-shirt and shorts.

'Okay,' she said chirpily, wriggling her bare nut-brown shoulders, 'I'm ready!'

He smiled at her. 'You look like a pixie!' he said.

'Come on mister, teach me to swim now. I can sort of dog paddle!'

They waded in till they were about tummy-deep. He took both her hands in his.

'It doesn't matter if you can dog paddle,' he said, 'we'll start from scratch, properly! Can you keep afloat? Can you feel the water trying to lift you up?'

She nodded.

'Great! Now lift up both your legs and sort of lie down in the water on your tummy. And start kicking your legs. Don't worry, I've got you!'

She nodded and did as he had instructed. He walked backwards, gently pulling her along.

'Okay, now, stand up in the water and start cycling and move your arms around like this. It's to keep you afloat!'

'Okay,' she spluttered, floating right up to him and straightening up.

'Great,' he said, 'you're doing great! But keep your mouth shut.'

'Umghfff!' she spluttered, suddenly out of her depth. 'Eek!' she squeaked as she went down and her head ducked under. She grabbed him and clung on to him.

'It's okay, I've got you!' he said, holding her firmly by her waist with both hands and lifting her up. 'Maybe we should get a tube next time!'

'Again!' she said gamely, 'I want to try that again!'

'Okay, come here,' he said, going to the rocky edge. 'You can hold on to the rock here and then kick your legs. I'll support you too. I'll show you how to breathe …'

From the edge, Djinn watched them, cocking his head this way and that. Brijesh held her horizontally as she kicked away valiantly, keeping her head out of the water and breathing noisily. Occasionally, he released his hold for the briefest moment.

'Right, now to breathing: take your head out of the water and take a deep breath. Now put your head under water and breathe out, either through your nose or mouth. You'll see bubbles. Repeat the process! And keep kicking those legs!'

'Yes, boss!' she said, flashing him a smile.

'Not bad,' he said fifteen minutes later. She stood up in the shallows and grinned mischievously at him. 'Sirji, can we fool around now?' she asked, splashing him with water. But she was impressed: he was thorough and didn't take anything for granted. She could dog paddle, sure, but could she swim properly? Probably not! So they had to start from scratch. She liked people like that.

They splashed each other, grinning and laughing, but he never tried to duck her or make her feel afraid or panic by dragging her to the deep end. At last, they waded out of the water. A pool was a great place to bond.

'Brrr!' she said, looking up. 'It's cold and cloudy again. These clothes are not going to dry and they'll wet our other clothes if we wear those over them!' The wind had picked up, hushing through the pines, sounding like the sea.

'Maybe we can go commando!' he said doubtfully.

'What's that?'

'We take these wet things off and put on our dry things. Then maybe we can make another fire and dry these off before putting them back on.'

'Oh … but …'

'Shut your eyes and promise not to peek,' he said, picking up his jeans.

'Okay!' She covered her eyes, but yet, couldn't resist leaving a teeny-weeny crack between her fingers. He had turned his back towards her and she caught just the glimpse of what she thought was a very cute brown butt. In seconds, he had yanked down his shorts and pulled up his jeans. He turned around.

'Okay, all clear! Now it's your turn!' Again, he turned his back to her.

'Don't you dare peek!' she warned. She stripped off her soaking T-shirt and shorts and bent down to pick up her overalls. A humongous, very hairy spider scuttled out from underneath and ran over her hand. She flailed her wrist frantically and the spider dropped away.

'Eek!' she shrieked, whipping her hand back, as Djinn barked and bounded over. 'Horrible spider, get off me!' Brijesh spun around and went scarlet. She was naked, still flailing her hand frantically.

'Wha … what?'

'A spider crawled up my hand … oh my God, don't *look*!'

He spun around again. 'Sorry!' he mumbled. Crap, he thought, he'd torn it! For a moment, there was only the hushing of the pines in the breeze. Then:

'Er … will you, will you please jhatka my overalls, there may be more spiders hiding in them,' she said in a small voice.

'Okay,' he said, 'toss them over to me!'

She leant down and tentatively picked up her overalls by a strap and chucked them across by his side. He picked them up and dusted them thoroughly, even inspecting the pockets. She waited, her arms across her chest. With his back still to her, he tossed the overalls over towards her.

'Okay, you can turn around now,' she told him, strapping her overalls over her bare shoulders. 'And thanks!' She glanced at him sideways.

She picked up her T-shirt and shorts and wrung them out. 'We'll go back to the beach and make another fire and dry these!' She looked up. 'Shoot, it looks like it's going to rain again in a bit.'

As the clouds wafted over silently, they built another fire on the beach and hung up their wet clothes on pine branches. With Djinn between them, they sat side by side, watching the flames.

'What's the time?' she asked, her chin on her drawn-up knees.

'Three-thirty.'

'They'll probably be pretty mad back at the house,' she grinned. 'But I don't care!'

'I had a good time,' he said softly. 'Thanks for showing me this place and *Rubadubdub* and all.'

'Next time, I'll take you all around the lake! We can bike nearly the whole way around it, almost right up to that stupid resort.'

'Okay. They've really built it in a stupid place.'

'We'd better start back in a little while,' she said, looking at the darkening sky.

'Have the clothes dried?' He felt his shorts. 'Still a bit damp, but not dripping!'

'Nani said you should never wear wet clothes when it's cold and windy!' She plucked her T-shirt off the line. 'Hmm ... but this seems okay, some parts are a bit damp but others are dry!' She turned her back to him and undid her overall buttons and wriggled into the T-shirt. 'It's good!' She stuffed her shorts into her backpack. 'Are you going to put on your shorts again?' she asked smiling mischievously.

'I guess I'll have to. I can hardly go back to the house holding them in my hand! I haven't got my backpack.'

'You could put them in mine,' she offered. He grinned wryly.

'Can you imagine what will happen if anyone finds my shorts in your backpack? They'll freak and throw me in the lake!'

She laughed. 'And you can bet that stupid Vinita Aunty and Meatloaf will want to search it the moment we get back! I stole their chocolates and cheese and energy bars, after all!'

'Okay, we'll give these ten minutes more and then I'm going to put them on!'

By the time they cast off, the sky was a deep, gunmetal grey. The wind had picked up too, raising wavelets on the lake.

'It's going to pour any minute,' Shoma said, 'and I forgot to bring an umbrella or raincoat! We're going to look like drowned rats today!'

Even as she spoke, a silvery sheen of rain swept across the lake and the first drops hit them squarely in their faces.

'So much for drying our clothes!' Brijesh said.

'Hey, we can shelter under the engine tarpaulin,' she said. 'It'll give us some protection! Djinn, you come here too!'

Brijesh moved up beside her. Djinn sat down between their feet as they unfolded the tarpaulin over their heads.

'Move up closer!' she said. 'It's a little small!'

It was fine for one person, not two: she was getting wet, holding the tarp over him so that he didn't.

'You're getting wet!' he said.

'It's okay!'

'No it's not! You'll get pneumonia and then your Nani will kill me!'

As if on cue, she sneezed.

'Listen, hop onto my lap – we'll take up less space that way,' he said.

'You don't mind?'

'No!'

But he could see she would have a problem trying to hold up the tarp and hop on to his lap at the same time.

'Okay, you hold up both ends of the tarp, yup, like that … and …'

He put his hands around her waist and effortlessly lifted her into his lap.

'There, so much better.'

She flashed him a shy smile.

'Thanks!'

'Okay, you hold up the left corner, while I steer. I can hold the right corner up. We'll have to hold it up high enough so we can see where we're going!'

'This is really freaky! We look like we're hiding behind a burqa!'

Brijesh wondered what anyone on the shore would think if they saw the *Rubadubdub* now. The rain drummed down on top of the tarpaulin but they remained relatively dry.

'I hope I'm not too heavy,' Shoma said, glancing at him. Her back was snug against his chest, her cheek against his. She could feel his warm breath on her cheek.

'No,' he said. 'You're a featherweight.'

The boat purred across the lake, bouncing lightly on the waves. In front of them, Big Djinn sat, quiet and stoic as ever. Quietly, Shoma raised her free right arm and put her hand over Brijesh's, holding up the tarp. And felt very contented as she entwined her fingers between his. Yes, she decided, she liked him very much indeed.

5

The rain had thinned into a fine drizzle by the time they reached the shore and moored the boat, covering it up again. Djinn shook himself vigorously, spraying a shower of silver droplets all over them.

'Djinn!' Shoma squealed, 'you wicked fellow!'

Brijesh looked at her and felt his own heart suddenly lurch. In the silvery, dark-cloud light, droplets of rain sparkled in her frizzy hair, illuminated like tiny pearls; her face was tanned nut brown but her cheeks, ears and nose flushed rosy pink, the tiny but beautiful diamond sparkled and her dark eyes danced with merriment. Tiny silver droplets pearled her earlobes.

'Let's go,' he said.

'Into the valley of death rode the two delinquents,' she chanted sotto voce, slipping her hand into his as they trudged homewards. It was mauve dark by the time they reached and the lights were on inside the house.

The birding group was in the drawing room. Shoma took a deep breath, squeezed Brijesh's hand and pushed open the door.

'Here goes!' she whispered.

The babble in the room died down as they all turned and stared at the pair.

'So the prodigal has returned,' Vinita Aunty announced sarcastically, raising her eyebrows, 'How nice of you to be so considerate and to have brought back Brijesh safely.'

'Budgie! Where have you been all day? Just look at you both!'

'Nani, I said I'd be back before dark and it's not dark yet.'

'Backchatting again! Young lady, I think we need an explanation and apology,' Vinita Aunty said, as Meatloaf nodded righteously. 'You were supposed to take us out in your boat this morning. We've been so worried all day.'

Liar! Shoma thought. You wouldn't give a rat's ass if we had drowned!

She looked straight at her aunt. 'I couldn't bear to do that.'

'What?'

'I couldn't bear to take a bunch of liars out in *Rubadubdub*.' She looked pointedly at her cousins and Zit-face and Bony Mouse.

The gang of four drew in their breath sharply.

'Shoma! Do you even know what you're saying? Apologize at once!'

'Apologize for telling the truth? Why?'

Her eyes flashed defiance but her heart was beating wildly. She had not been in the room for two minutes and matters had already gone out of hand! Her aunt really knew how to wind her up! Beside her, Brijesh stood stock still, his heart beating fast.

Vinita Aunty, Meatloaf and Sohan Uncle exchanged stunned looks. The gang of four just goggled and gasped. Nani's hands were in front of her face.

'Ma, do you hear this?' Vinita Aunty said tearfully, as if she had been personally insulted. 'Did you hear what she just said? And yet you defend her! I've never heard such rudeness in my life!'

Sohan Uncle cleared his throat and tried laying down the law. 'Shoma, until further notice—and certainly until you have apologized for your behaviour and to your cousins— you are forbidden to ride your bicycle and take out your boat. Is that clear?'

'You can't forbid me anything, you're not my father! Besides, you'll never find my bike or boat, so there!'

Sohan Uncle took a step back gaping like the fish they had caught and eaten.

'Budgie … please, say you're sorry …' Nani was almost in tears.

'Nani, why should I? You always said I should tell the truth. Well, I have, so why should I say sorry?'

'Well, you are grounded!' Vinita Aunty was going red in the face. She stood up and pointed to the door. 'You will go to your room immediately and stay there until you apologize.

Your meals of bread and water will be sent up to you. If your parents can't be bothered to discipline you, someone else will have to.'

Shoma shook her head. 'I can't. Zit-face and Bony Mouse are staying in my room, remember?'

'Zit-what? So, now you're insulting your guests too.' Vinita Aunty breathed deeply. 'Arvind, Kalpana, take your things and shift to your father's room – you'll have to tolerate his snoring, I'm afraid. Shoma is to go to her room and stay there.'

She strode forth and grabbed Shoma by the arm. 'Come on, young lady, march!'

Shoma tugged but Vinita Aunty's grip was vice-like.

'Leave me alone! Get off my case, will you?' she squealed. 'You're hurting me. Let me go, you ugly old billy-goat!'

There was stunned silence. Brijesh's eyes widened. Oh crap, he thought, she's really done it this time! But a part of him glowed with admiration: what a kid! She had more guts than he would ever have.

'What ... did ... you ... say?'

Even Shoma knew that this time she had gone too far.

'I'm sorry!' she said quickly, but also aware that now she was lying. 'I take that back.'

'Did you hear what she called me?' Vinita Aunty looked like she was about to have a stroke and give herself a hernia at the same time. 'Repeat that!'

Shoma shook her head. 'I said I'm sorry.'

'Repeat it! What did you just call me? Let everyone hear.'

She was surrounded by Vinita Aunty, Sohan Uncle and Meatloaf. Professor Damodar remained seated on the sofa and lit his pipe, not quite knowing what to make of the drama. The gang of four's mouths had fallen open. Nani was shaking her head and twisting a handkerchief in her hands. Poor Brijesh didn't know what to do or where to look. Vinita Aunty shook Shoma.

'Repeat it, I said!' she hissed.

Shoma just shook her head, the tears beginning to spurt from her eyes. This had all gone way out of control. Brijesh cleared his throat tentatively.

'Um ... actually it was my idea to go out in the boat,' he mumbled. 'I ... I asked her to take me ...'

They looked at him incredulously: they weren't buying it. Shoma stared at him astounded, a tiny warm flicker of light beginning to glow deep inside her. What an ass he was! As if they'd believe him for even a second. But still ...

'Brijesh, please stay out of this. Why don't you go to your room until we sort this out?' Vinita Aunty said tersely. She turned her attention back to Shoma.

'Come on, you little minx; up to your room – and stay there!'

Ignominiously, she dragged Shoma up the stairs. She had a pincer-like grip. Behind her, Zit-face and Bony Mouse hurried up to collect their cases and toothbrushes. Breathing deeply, Vinita Aunty waited outside as they packed, her fingers tightly clamped around Shoma's arm.

'Your parents have taught you nothing!' she sneered.
'There's no point even complaining to them. They couldn't
care less what you turned out to be!'

'They do care!'

Zit-face and Bony Mouse hurried out with their luggage.

'Now get in!' Vinita Aunty snapped, pushing her in and
slamming the door and turning the key. 'Your dinner will be
sent up to you.'

Shoma shook her head dazedly and walked slowly to
her bed, not believing what had just happened. Slowly, she
put down her backpack and sat on her bed. No! She would
not cry. Well, at least she had her room back. She stripped
the sheets off her bed and dusted them down to get rid
of any biscuit crumbs that might have still been on them.
Then she dampened a cloth and vigorously wiped the head-
rest where Zit-face had rested his oily head. She checked
her backpack: she still had an apple and a pear left, so she
wouldn't go hungry.

Downstairs, after an awkward silence, the conversation
began again.

'Really, ma, you'll have to do something about that girl,'
Vinita Aunty said. 'She's going to turn out to be a real bad
penny otherwise. In two or three years, she'll be mixing
with bad company! As it is, she hijacked poor Brijesh for the
whole day today.'

Nani shook her head. 'I don't understand. She's not at
all like this when you all are not here. I don't know what

happens. She just speaks her mind. And Shoma has never lied …'

Vinita Aunty flushed angrily. 'Are you saying that Aditi and all the others are lying then?'

'No, no … of course not, but …'

'But that girl needs to be taught a lesson. Keep her on bread and water and up in her room for a couple of days and she'll apologize. She must apologize.'

Nani shook her head worriedly. 'I don't think she will. Shoma is a very proud girl. She's as stubborn as Ramona.'

'Well, she will have to!' Vinita Aunty shook her head. 'Otherwise, ma, we'll go and stay somewhere else. At least our kids won't be in danger of being attacked and having their eyes scratched out!'

'No, no … please …'

Poor Nani had had a very trying day indeed and the last thing she wanted was more upheaval and trouble. Late that morning, the motorboat from the resort had purred up to the lake shore again and Shri Suraj Mukhi and four associates had made their way up to the house.

'Hello-ji, what can I do for you all?' Nani asked them hospitably, wondering what the hell the men wanted.

The four associates looked around warily. 'Kutta bandha hain?' one asked.

Nani smiled, 'The children have taken the dog out; it's all right!'

Shri Mukhi was setting up a laptop on the dining table.

'Madam,' he said, 'we just wanted to show you what this place would look like after we have devloped it. Provided, of course, you sell the property to us.' He smiled and nodded as if that were a foregone conclusion. 'It is, of course, an artist's impression, but the finished product will be 99 per cent the same. See here, we have docks for speedboats and yachts, a smooth promenade leading around the lake. Each of these villas will have a lakeside view and its own Jacuzzi and gym and yoga room. There will be a clubhouse with a card room and billiards table and ...'

Nani had stared in horror as the presentation unfolded slide by slide.

'Shri Mukhiji,' she said quietly, 'this property is not for sale. In any case, I think what you have done to the mountain on the other side of the lake is nothing short of sacrilege. A desecration! That whole mountain must have become unstable!'

'No, no, madamji, you can't believe that! Look at the greenery! It's a golf course designed by a professional golfer ...'

'You cut down thousands of trees – and as one writer put it so well, a golf course is nature neutered! It's like bringing the outdoors indoors!'

'Eh? But madam, we are only making nature safe for all people to enjoy. In the forests there are bears and leopards and snakes and poisonous insects and plants ...'

'That's their home. We have our cities and towns.'

'Yes, yes, but we humans must also commune with nature! But nature is wild and dangerous, so we must tame it and trim it a bit.'

'If you ask me, Shri Mukhiji, what you have done to that mountain is very dangerous indeed. You've made the entire mountainside unstable by taking out all the trees and artificially bolstering up the slope. And I'm sorry, but this property is not for sale.'

Shri Mukhiji folded up his laptop and shrugged.

'No problem, madam, but if you have a change of heart, please get in touch! I wanted to warn you also – you know, a bear attacked a child on our side of the mountain. My fellows tell me your little granddaughter runs around in the forests all by herself. It's the second or third bear attack that's been reported from this area. Also, a leopard was seen at the edge of the golf course with a pet dog in its mouth ...'

'Shoma has her dog to protect her. Big Djinn is quite capable of tackling a leopard and looking after her. But thank you for telling me, I'll tell Shoma to be careful.'

Shri Mukhiji made a final pitch and opened his laptop again. 'Madamji, do reconsider: the project will be so good for the economy of this place. With smooth roads, you won't need to use donkeys to ferry supplies and people to and fro.' He pointed to a slide that had just appeared and rubbed his hands.

'Ah, this is the villa we had designed specially for you and your family! It's the biggest, most luxurious one and overlooks the lake.'

'Thank you, ji, but as I said, this property is not for sale.'

'Very well, ji, we'll take our leave now. Thank you for your time.'

'You're welcome,' Nani said, sighing with relief.

At the top of the steps leading down to the garden and meadow, Shri Mukhiji turned around and said again, 'And do warn your granddaughter about the bear ...'

'I will, and thank you.'

The whole encounter had been a little disturbing and left her vaguely uneasy. And now she had to deal with this huge family fracas that had blown up in her face.

In the cabin of the blue and white motorboat, Shri Mukhiji's expression was grim. He summoned his chief aide with a finger and gave his orders. The man nodded impassively.

'Jee sahib, but if we do it like that it will be obvious ...'

Shri Mukhiji nodded. 'It will be obvious – that is the intention. But it will be unprovable. No one insults Shri Suraj Mukhi and gets away with it. A desecration indeed! The buddhi will be taught a lesson she will never forget!'

And now Nani was trying to deal with the family. Siddharth shook his head. 'What I can't believe,' he said in that sanctimonious tone that grated even on Nani's nerves, 'is that Shoma's just not interested and makes fun of those who are ...'

'Siddharth, everyone need not be interested in birds as you all are. Shoma is interested in other things, like her mountain bike and boat and painting and ...'

'Nani, we've seen her paintings,' Aditi said, shaking her head, 'Really gross!'

'Okay, let's talk about something else,' Vinita Aunty said, shaking her head. 'Siddharth darling, let's see those beautiful slides again, shall we?'

Aditi got to her feet. 'I'll just fetch Brijesh. The poor guy must be feeling so left out and embarrassed!' She knocked on Brijesh's door and pushed it open and then backed away, alarmed, as the huge shaggy dog at Brijesh's bedside rose to his feet with a growl. Right after backing away from Shoma's room, Brijesh had sneaked out of the back door and brought Djinn inside. It had started pouring again, and was windy and cold. Rain-spray would soak the verandah. Also, the presence of the big dog was comforting. Brijesh had been working on his plane when Aditi had barged in.

'Oh, oh!' Aditi squeaked, her eyes on Djinn. 'We're watching Siddharth's bird slides downstairs,' she said, 'Nani asked if you would like to join us!'

'Umm ... I'm fine here; I want to finish building this,' he said, 'thanks!'

Disappointed, Aditi went back down, but there was a glint in her eye.

Siddharth set up his laptop and Sohan Uncle fiddled with the overhead projector.

'Papa, should we keep the best recordings for the beginning of the show or the end?' he asked.

'Divide them up. Then people will stay right from the beginning and won't mind waiting till the end.'

'Okay, then maybe we can start off with the white-rumped shama … that'll make them sit up.'

Half an hour later, Nani announced dinner; another lavish spread of biryani and fish curry and fresh vegetables. Once again, Aditi traipsed upstairs and knocked on Brijesh's door. 'Dinner!' she called. Brijesh came down, with Djinn by his side, whom Kusum quickly took to the kitchen.

'Djinn seems to like you,' Nani said, smiling. As they took their places at the table, she picked up Shoma's plate and began filling it up.

'Ma, what are you doing?' Vinita Aunty's eyes bulged.

'Taking something up for Budgie! God knows what she's eaten all day. She must be famished.'

'She stole a whole lot of our stuff from the fridge, Nani,' Aditi said, sitting down primly. 'She couldn't be that hungry.'

Vinita Aunty took the plate out of Nani's hands, shaking her head. 'Bread and water,' she said. 'That girl must know we are serious.'

'I'll get it and take it up,' Meatloaf offered.

She took a stainless steel thali with one slice of dry bread and a tumbler of water and went up the stairs and knocked on the door.

'Who is it?' Shoma called sullenly.

'It's me, Charulata Aunty. I've brought your dinner up. Of course, if you apologize, you can come down and join us. We're having biryani and fish curry and it's quite delicious.'

'Leave the tray and go away.'

'Shoma …'

'Go away!'

'Oh well, as you wish …' Meatloaf unlocked the door and gingerly left the thali and tumbler just inside the room. It was quite dark, and she was afraid of how Shoma might react. But it was all quiet and she quickly withdrew.

Shoma stared at the thali. A solitary slice of dry bread and a tumbler of water … Her dinner after a whole day's outing. The fish, energy bars, chocolate and cheese had been digested long ago. She was famished. A flame of anger blazed. She picked up the thali and flung it through the window grille, followed by the tumbler. Then she slammed the window and ran back to her bed, her face flushed with anger.

The thali and tumbler clanged horribly in the patio, just outside the dining room, startling the group at the table. Vinita Aunty shook her head grimly.

'Another tantrum!' said Meatloaf. 'Now she's throwing good food out of the window! Well, don't worry, she'll learn eventually.'

Vinita Aunty nodded.

'They all do,' she said, chillingly, 'nothing like a bit of starvation to bring a delinquent to heel!'

'Okay, so where should we go tomorrow morning?' Vinita Aunty went on brightly, as if nothing at all were the matter.

'Let's make it a whole day's outing,' Meatloaf said. 'Once the seminar starts we won't be able to get away. Let's go right around the lake.'

'Right! I'll tell Kusum to organize our breakfast and lunch.' She looked down the table. 'Ma,' she said solicitously, 'you're hardly eating anything.'

'I'm just too upset to eat,' Nani said. 'Maybe I should go and talk to Shoma. You know I have to go to Nainital tomorrow for a few days ...' Nani had some urgent work with her lawyers that needed attending to. How would her little Budgie manage alone with this lot during her absence, she wondered. She'd better tell her to try and keep a cool head and stay out of the Vermas' hair.

'Just let her be, ma!' Vinita Aunty said, 'She'll just throw another tantrum.'

Brijesh put his head down and silently ate his dinner. Suddenly, he was tired and badly missed his mother. He didn't need to be entangled in the nasty quarrels of another family. But yes, Budgie and Big Djinn – they were something else, weren't they? Perhaps he ought to sneak out and check on her after everyone had gone to bed. Maybe he could take her something to eat.

Shoma pressed her ear to her bedroom door and listened. It seemed all quiet, as if the birders had all gone to bed. It was just after ten and she was absolutely ravenous; the fragrant aroma of biryani and fish curry had swirled up from under the door and driven her nearly crazy. She peered through the keyhole. Yes, thank God, the key was still there. She had read about how one could open the door by dropping the key on a piece of paper and then pulling it ...

In their bedroom with their parents, Siddharth and Aditi prepared for bed too. Then Aditi, who had just lain down, suddenly sat up.

'Mama, do you have the key to the door of Shoma's room?'

Her mother looked at her in surprise. 'No, it's in the keyhole.'

Aditi smiled; it was not a very nice smile. 'Mama, then Shoma will definitely try and get out.' Actually, another awful thought had struck her: what if Brijesh let her out, or went to her? After all, they had spent the whole day together …

'How?' Vinita Aunty asked. 'She can't. That door is solid oak.'

'Mama! All she has to do is push the key out of its hole onto a piece of paper slipped under the door and then draw it back in. It's an old trick.'

'Oh? Is that so? Then I think you should go and get the key.'

'Sure, mama!' Aditi jumped out of bed quickly, followed by Siddharth.

'Look,' she whispered as they reached the hall. 'We're just in time …'

A sheet of paper was being thrust out from under the door.

'Siddharth, go and call mama and papa and Damodar Uncle and the others. But don't disturb Nani. This is going to be such fun!'

What they didn't notice was that Brijesh's door too had opened. He saw them and retreated at once. He'd left it too late!

'Okay,' Shoma whispered to herself, 'now to drop the key. Hope it stays on the paper!' She took a compass and began jiggling it in the hole. The key, a heavy brass one, resisted. Shoma jiggled some more and suddenly felt the key come free. She pushed the compass in a little more, very carefully, and heard the key drop with a muffled clunk as it landed on the paper.

'Great!' Shoma bent right down and peered under the crack. Lo and behold, she could see the key on the paper. 'Okay, now slowly, slowly, catch the monkey ...' she whispered gleefully. 'That stupid Vinita Aunty can go and suck eggs! Hah!'

Inch by inch she pulled the piece of paper back. Luckily, the gap between the floor and the bottom of the door was quite large and the key slid through without a problem. She grabbed it, grinning, and unlocked the door.

'Going somewhere, Shoma?' Vinita Aunty inquired icily, standing just outside the door, her hands on her hips. Behind her, in a semi-circle, stood all the others, grinning at her. 'Aditi knew you'd try this and I see we're just in time.'

A ripple of sniggering laughter went through the onlookers. Aditi nudged Bony Mouse who nudged Zit-face who nudged Siddharth. Sohan Uncle was shaking his head at Meatloaf. At the end of the corridor, Brijesh stood at his door and watched. Now what?

Shoma felt her face go hot and red with shame. She had been royally humiliated in front of everyone yet again; they were all laughing at her. Vinita Aunty stepped forward.

'Why can't you do as you're told?' she snapped. She reached inside the door and took out the key. 'Now get back in and stay there!' She grabbed Shoma's arm and thrust her inside.

'Sorry, Shoma, your great escape didn't work!' Aditi couldn't help gloating. 'I knew you'd try something slimy like this.'

Very near tears, Shoma grabbed the door and slammed it shut in their faces, hearing their ripple of laughter yet again. She ran to her bed and lay face down, as the sobs burst through. She hardly heard the key turn in the lock. This time, of course, the key would not stay there.

Minutes later, there was a soft knock on the door.

'Budgie?' It was Brijesh.

'Go away. I hate all of you ... What do you want?'

'Are you okay? I wanted to bring you some food, but she's gone and locked the door and taken away the key!' Down the long corridor, another door opened.

'Got to go!' he said hurriedly, 'someone's coming!' He slipped back into his room.

This time it was Nani, who had awoken when Shoma had slammed the door. She had planned to let Shoma into her bedroom, after the others had gone to bed, but had drifted off herself. And now she didn't want to confront that aggressive Vinita again tonight.

'Budgie, are you okay? I wanted you to sleep in my room, but the key's gone. And you know you lost the duplicate …'

'Vinita Aunty has the key.'

'Budgie, it's very late. I can't disturb her now. Try and sleep, okay? I'll get her to open the door first thing tomorrow morning. And listen, darling, I have to go to Nainital tomorrow for a few days on work. Budgie, try to stay out of their way and don't let there be more trouble. Are you very hungry, sweetie?'

'It's okay, Nani,' Shoma said in a small voice. 'I still have an apple and a pear left.' She bit into the apple. 'You're going away for how many days?'

'I don't know, darling, but I have to go.'

Early next morning, Aditi knocked on Brijesh's door once again, accompanied by Siddharth this time.

'Brijesh, wake up and get dressed! We're going birding for the day!' There was no response. They knocked again, louder. Still nothing. They tried pushing it open, but it did not budge. Under the duvet, Brijesh shut his eyes, covered his ears with a pillow and waited.

'He's locked it!'

'And he sleeps like the dead! Besides, that wolf might be there. Too bad. Come on, let's go!' Siddharth said. He went back down, reluctantly followed by his sister. Brijesh breathed a sigh of relief and dozed off.

But for Shoma, things became much worse the next morning. The birding group had left the house before Nani had awoken. She was absolutely horrified when she got up about an hour later. She had to leave soon. She tried Shoma's door and found it locked, and there was no sign of the key. There was a terse note from Vinita saying they'd be back in the evening, with no mention of Shoma. At seven, Shoma awoke and hammered on the door.

'Nani!' she called. 'Nani, open the door!'

'Budgie, they've gone out for the whole day and taken the key with them,' Nani said, vexed, eyeing the door. It was solid oak and the lock was very strong. There was no way that anyone could break it down. Brijesh's door opened and he joined her.

'Good morning, Brijesh,' Nani said.

'Good morning.' He pointed to the door. 'Shoma's still locked inside?'

'Yes. And Vinita's taken the key with her!'

From inside, Shoma asked, 'Nani, what did you say?'

'Don't worry, dear. I'll send Kusum after them. She can get the key from Vinita Aunty and give it to Brijesh. He's here. I have to leave for Nainital in a little while!'

She sent Kusum off, with a note, *'Vinita, you forgot to leave the key to Shoma's door. Please give it to Kusum.'* It took poor Kusum over an hour to locate the group. Vinita Aunty read the note and shook her head.

'Badi memsahib ko bolo Shoma kamre may rahegi. Tell memsahib that Shoma is to remain in her room all day. We'll see in the evening.'

Kusum had still not returned when Nani got onto Grumpy to begin the ride over the ridge to the car park.

'Brijesh, keep her company, will you?' she asked. He nodded, Djinn again by his side.

'Sure, Aunty. You know … she didn't tell you but Aditi deliberately spilled Coke on her paintings and the others did lie to cover up. That's why she refused to apologize!'

'Oh my God! The poor little thing! I'll … I'll talk to Vinita Aunty when I get back,' Nani said. But for the first time, a slow anger had begun to burn inside her. No one had the right to treat her Budgie like this.

Brijesh waved Nani goodbye and went back in with Djinn. The house was quiet. He took a chair and sat down outside Shoma's room.

'Hey, Shoma, I'm still here,' he said tentatively.

'You didn't go with them?'

'Nah – I refused to wake up!'

'Can you open the door?'

'No. Your aunt wouldn't give Kusum Didi the key. She told her you'd have to wait till the evening, when they get back.'

'But I've finished the apple and pear and I'm hungry!'

It was only nine o'clock in the morning. The whole day stretched ahead; she would be weak with hunger and thirst by the evening.

Brijesh frowned. 'Shoma, your room does have a window, doesn't it?'

'Yes, of course! But it has a grille fixed inside, so I can't climb out of it!'

'No, I guess not. But I suppose Kusum Didi would have a nylon rope? You know, like a clothesline?'

'Yes, of course!'

'Okay, here's what we can do. I'll tie a pebble to the rope and throw it up through the window grille. You pull it in, and tie it to something. Then we'll tie a tiffin box to the other end, and you can haul it up. At least, you won't go hungry!'

'You're a genius!' she said, enthused. 'Actually, Annie has a catapult to scare away the monkeys. You can shoot the pebble through the window with that.'

To Brijesh's delight, Kusum and Annie were more than happy to be co-conspirators in his scheme. Neither of them liked either Vinita Aunty or Meatloaf.

'*Hum ekdum khana garam karta hain, baba!* I'll heat the food up straightaway, baba,' Kusum chuckled, her sloe eyes sparkling shrewdly as she patted Brijesh's cheek. '*Ek din me, Shoma baby ke saath reh ke aapka gaal lal ho gaya – lagta hain aap ko usse pyaar ho raha hain!* You've got rosy cheeks in one day after being with Shoma baby!' she teased him. Brijesh felt his cheeks go warm and red.

They had to tie the pebble to a thinner length of twine, which in turn was tied to the nylon clothesline. Annie handed Brijesh the steel and wood catapult. As Djinn watched interestedly, he took aim.

'Keep away from the window, Shoma,' he shouted, 'incoming!'

The first two times the pebble just bounced off the grille. But the third time it went straight through.

'Djinn, we're in!' he exulted as the dog thumped his tail. They tied the tiffin box to the rope and carefully Shoma pulled it up. It was just big enough to fit through the curly wrought-iron grille. Brijesh grinned, realizing that this was perhaps the first time he had actually felt happy since his mom had died. He went to the fridge and took out a big bar of Toblerone and a box of expensive Lindt chocolates that Vinita Aunty and family had brought with them.

Up in her room, Shoma ate hungrily.

'This is great!' she called down. 'Thanks so much!'

'Send down the box again and I'll send you some stolen chocolate,' he said, 'and some gulab jamuns!'

But Shoma was still a prisoner in her own room, for the whole day. How the hell would she pass the time?

'Hey, I'm back here, with Djinn,' Brijesh said after he had bathed and changed and had breakfast. 'How do you want to spend the day?'

'I don't know. I'll finish off my paintings properly, I guess. But it's not fair!'

'Ya, tell me about it!' It had not been fair at all that his mom had died. 'I know what you mean!'

'You're sweet, Bridge! Maybe you should take Djinn for a walk. Don't stay cooped up in the corridor all day.'

'No, it's okay.'

Brijesh sat quietly outside and actually dared to stroke Djinn for once. The huge dog put his ears back and closed his eyes.

'Hey!' he said, elated, 'Djinn's letting me pet him!'

'I told you he likes you!'

He could hear Shoma clatter her painting things around and then start whistling as she worked.

'Hey,' she said suddenly, 'Bridge, are you still there?'

'Yes!'

'Guess what I found? I pinched Siddharth's MP3 recorder yesterday evening! I'm going to erase everything and record rude farty noises in their place!'

'Shoma, you'll get into more trouble!'

'Can't be worse than this!'

She plugged in the earphones and turned the recording on to the last item. Her eyes grew round as she overheard the conversation her grandmother had had with Shri Suraj Mukhi during his first 'courtesy call'.

'Oh my God!' she hissed, 'Brijesh, that Suraj Mukhi fellow wants to buy our house and build another resort here!'

'What?'

'Ya, it's all been recorded. But Nani's refused!' She giggled. 'He even said that I should be careful of bears and leopards while going around!'

'He sounds nuts!'

'Bonkers! Now let me see what else there is ... Oh, they're all bird calls.' She grinned mischievously. 'I'll connect the player to my speakers so you can hear them through the door too!'

Through the door, he could hear the bird-call recordings. Several of the lovely bird calls reminded him of her whistling.

Something wicked went click, click, click in Brijesh's brain and a sudden crafty grin lit up his face.

'Shoma, listen! Do you really want to get your own back on all of them?'

'Of course! Why?'

'Then listen!' He put his mouth to the door and outlined his idea. 'What do you think? Worth a shot?'

'Brijesh, you're a genius! But now I'll have to practice all day!'

'Sure! But you're pretty good already.'

'Okay, then you listen and tell me what you like!'

He grinned as he heard her whistling tunefully through the door.

6

The birding group returned at six that evening, tired and crabby and tracking muddy shoes all over Nani's polished wooden floors. A little brown bird had caused a rift in the ranks: while Vinita Aunty, Sohan Uncle and their kids had thought it to be of a particular species, Meatloaf and Professor Damodar and their kids had disagreed.

'Of course, it had a dark supercilium,' Vinita Aunty declared, 'it was quite clear.'

'Vinita, you must have imagined it,' Meatloaf said. 'It must have been the shadow of a branch or something.'

'I think I know the difference between a branch's shadow and a bird's supercilium.' Vinita Aunty strode into the kitchen. 'Kusum,' she yelled, 'chai lao!'

Kusum came out of the kitchen just as Brijesh came down the stairs with Djinn at his side. The big dog seemed to have adopted him.

'*Jee memsahib, par Shoma baby ka kamre ka chaabi dena — badi memsahib ne kaha.* Certainly, madam, but first give me the key to Shoma baby's room. Those are Madam's instructions.'

Vinita Aunty looked affronted.

Brijesh cleared his throat. 'Aunty, she's been up there all day – she must be famished!'

Vinita Aunty looked at him coldly. 'She has only herself to blame for that! Is she ready to apologize?'

She stomped upstairs followed by the others, including Brijesh and Kusum.

They crowded in the doorway as Vinita Aunty unlocked the door and entered. Shoma was lying on her bed, her hands behind her head. She stared at them coolly.

'So are you ready to say you're sorry?' Vinita Aunty's hands were on her hips, her head cocked aggressively to one side, like a fighting cockerel.

'Baby, what will you have to eat?' Kusum asked as she went up to her and stroked her head. 'You must be very hungry!' Kusum winked and Brijesh hid a grin.

'Kusum, she has to apologize first.'

'I'd like some French toast, please, Kusum Didi,' Shoma replied, looking pointedly at Vinita Aunty. 'I'm feeling very weak.'

'*Abhi banaata baby!* I'll make it just now, baby!' Kusum said. At the door, Brijesh quietly removed the key from the keyhole and palmed it, his heart beating fast. He slipped the key to Kusum as she passed him. Her wrinkled hand closed over it as she smiled at him and scurried down the stairs.

'So are you going to apologize or do you want to spend another day here?'

'Aunty, I said sorry to you.'

'To Aditi and the others – they deserve an apology too …'

Shoma shook her head stubbornly. 'I don't say sorry to liars. I told you.'

'Again, the same thing! What's wrong with you? Why are you so stubborn? Just like your mother! Very well, you can spend tomorrow here too.'

Shoma just couldn't help herself. She smiled sweetly at her aunt. 'What's for dinner, Aunty?' she asked. 'Yesterday's biryani and fish curry and gulab jamuns were delicious!'

'You! You cheeky little thing! Backchatting again!'

Vinita Aunty really looked like she was going to explode and Aditi and Siddharth tried to look pained. Zit-face and Bony Mouse had gone down to join Sohan Uncle and Professor Damodar, who had prudently decided to remain downstairs. Meatloaf was still in a huff over the little brown bird.

'Kusum can make as many French toasts as she wants but you're not having a morsel until you apologize, is that clear?' Vinita Aunty backed out and shut the door and then realized the key was missing.

'Where's the key? Who's taken it?' She glared at poor Brijesh. He shook his head.

'I don't have it, Aunty,' he said.

Vinita Aunty slammed the door shut and pounded down the stairs.

'Kusum!' she bellowed, 'Kusum!'

'Jee memsahib?' Kusum emerged from the kitchen with a heap of fragrant French toast on a plate, the light of battle in her eyes. Vinita Aunty held out her hand.

'*Chaabi*! The key!'

At the bottom of the stairs, Brijesh watched with bated breath. Kusum's eyes flashed angrily.

'*Badi memsahib ka order hain, baby kamre me lock nahin hoaga!* It is Madam's order that baby will not be locked in her room! She's been locked all day and hasn't eaten anything, and she's just a child!' It was a battle Vinita Aunty knew she was not going to win.

'Very well, you all may go on spoiling her sick. Come on, kids – and listen to me. None of you are to talk or have anything to do with Shoma for the rest of our stay here. Do you understand?'

'Yes, mama.'

Shoma had followed them down the stairs and was now standing behind Brijesh. She just couldn't control her tongue – yet again.

'Oh, that's great. Actually, I might go out in *Rubadubdub* tomorrow, if it's not raining. Would you like to come along with me again, Bridge?' She grinned wickedly at him. 'You know, we can drift really close to the birds without disturbing them …'

Dinner was absolutely wonderful – from Shoma's point of view at least. As they settled in their places the others began their usual bird babble, still arguing about the little brown bird.

'Excuse me,' Shoma said to Aditi with exquisite politeness.

'Could you pass me the salt and pepper, please?'

Glowering, Aditi did so, after glancing at her mother.

'Thank you so much!' She smiled at Siddharth. 'Siddharth, did you manage to record the calls of any new birds today?' she inquired, biting her cheeks.

Siddharth ignored her and stabbed at his chicken thigh.

Shoma shrugged. 'Oh well, too bad …' She looked at Kusum who was hovering over them. 'Kusum Didi, this chicken is absolutely delicious, just like last night's biryani!'

'Thank you, baby.'

She turned to Zit-face and Bony Mouse. 'I hope you both are enjoying your stay,' she said, hospitably. 'But do check yourself for leeches and ticks when you return from an outing. Sometimes they can get into really bad places.' She nodded knowingly and turned to Aditi again.

'Aditi, do you have leeches in England? Everyone says it rains a lot there.'

Aditi attacked her plate ferociously.

Vinita Aunty turned to Shoma furiously. 'Have you finished prattling?' she asked bitingly. Shoma looked hurt.

'Aunty, I was just asking a few harmless questions, that's all.'

'You are insubordinate and rude!'

'I was just telling them to be careful about leeches. They can get into awkward places and bleed you white, and you won't even know.' She smiled sweetly again. 'Like Dracula, you know!'

Vinita Aunty took a deep breath and counted till ten. She turned to the others.

'So, should we go out tomorrow morning before heading for the seminar?' she asked brightly, her face red. 'We might see something unusual!'

'Let's go to the stream again at about six,' Siddharth said. 'I'm hoping to record the grey-winged blackbird – that'll be a real feather in my cap.' He looked around the table. 'You know, apart from all our local top-shot birders, Sir Harold Radcliffe will also be attending some of the sessions. I hope he'll stay for mine. Maybe he'll take me out birding when we get back to England.'

'Who's he?' Shoma asked interestedly.

'He's ...' Siddharth began and then shut up and looked guiltily at his mother.

'Oh, I get it, must be some bird-watching heavy who's seen all the birds in the world at least twelve times.' Shoma nodded. 'Well, best of luck, Siddharth, I hope you can show off to him.'

Vinita Aunty and Meatloaf both made noises that sounded like some very unpleasant angry animal stuck in a drain.

'Aunty, what? I'm just trying to make polite conversation. You always say I should try to be interested.' She sniffed meaningfully. 'Of course, it would help if some people were polite enough to reply to my questions.'

'Excuse me!' Brijesh vacated his place with alacrity and went into the drawing room.

'I'd better see that he's all right,' Shoma said, smiling sadly. 'He's just lost his mother, poor fellow!'

In the drawing room, she found Brijesh standing with his back to the dining room, his shoulders shaking. For a moment, she was alarmed. Oh, God, was he really crying?

'Hey, Bridge ... are you okay?'

He turned. He did have tears in his eyes, spilling down his cheeks.

'Are you laughing or crying?' she asked, because she honestly couldn't tell.

He looked at her. 'I don't know! You ... you're totally over the top, nuts; you really wind up your aunt like a clockwork toy. It makes me laugh and then I feel guilty because I'm laughing and mom's just died and then I feel like crying ...'

'I don't think your mom would have wanted you to cry all the time. She'd want you to laugh!'

He stared at her and wiped his face.

'I ... I guess you're right,' he said thickly.

'They're really funny,' Shoma went on, deadpan. 'All they talk about is birds, but when you ask them questions about birds, they clam up! How will I learn if my questions aren't answered?'

'You are one of a kind,' Brijesh said, a crooked grin on his face. 'Nuts!'

'Come on, we'd better go back before they finish the halwa.'

At about 10 p.m., bathed and changed and ready for bed, Shoma came down to say goodnight to Big Djinn. The hateful birding group was still in the drawing room, animatedly arguing as usual. But, yet again, Djinn was AWOL from the verandah and his bed. 'Oh,' she exclaimed, 'the fellow must be with Bridge again; he really likes him!' Just then the phone rang, startling everyone. Shoma grabbed it. It was Nani, calling to check that all was well.

'Nani, I'm fine! Brijesh and Kusum Didi took away the key so Vinita Aunty couldn't lock me back in again as she wanted to!' Shoma tattled loudly as Vinita Aunty looked daggers at her. She strode over and snatched the receiver from Shoma. Shoma backed away, then snuck up the stairs and picked up the extension in Nani's bedroom. Vinita Aunty was letting off steam.

'Ma, Shoma is just impossible. Rude and cheeky! I've told the other kids not to speak to her until she apologizes! She needs a good spanking, if you ask me!'

'Vinita, what Aditi told Shoma about her parents was cruel and hurtful. Budgie was very upset. I think you might have a little chat with Aditi about it!' A steely note had entered Nani's voice. 'Or I will, when I get back!'

'Ma, Aditi darling was only repeating what I had said.'

'Then you should be ashamed of yourself, Vinita! What a thing to say!'

'Ma, this is all too much. When are you getting back?'

'In three or four days, or maybe a week. I have to finish Brijesh's work ...'

'Oh – and we're going to have to put up with Shoma's rudeness all that while?'

'Try not to wind her up! Goodbye, dear!'

Shoma smiled prettily and stuck out her tongue as she put the receiver down and left the room. Softly, she knocked on Brijesh's door.

'Come in!'

Djinn looked up from the base of Brijesh's bed and thumped his tail.

'It looks like he's adopted you,' she said, smiling, 'he's never been like that with anyone!' He shrugged. He was bent over the table, working on his model. There were coloured wires all over, spewing out of various parts of the plane.

'Wow!' she said, astonished, 'it's really beautiful!' The model was almost complete, and pretty large: its wingspan must have been close to five feet! Most of it had already been painted olive green.

'Will it fly?' she asked.

He nodded. 'Of course!'

'What are you doing now?'

'Installing the wiring harnesses!' He looked up. 'She's got four engines and two cameras too – one on the bomb bay underneath and one in the cockpit.'

'What is it?'

He smiled proudly. 'She's a World War II Lancaster bomber. Mom's nana actually flew one of these during the War. I was thinking we could take it to the island and fly it from that grassy place on top. The ground there was very smooth and flat, perfect for a runway.'

'When will she be ready to fly?'

'Tomorrow or the day after! I have to test the engines and see that all the controls respond properly to commands from the control unit.'

'Wow!' She was impressed. 'Do the engines run on petrol?'

He glanced at her and grinned. 'Batteries! But the motors are pretty powerful. She'll fly for 15 or 20 minutes depending on the wind.'

He got back to work, frowning as he bent over the plane. She glanced at the model, lying there patiently on the table, as he worked carefully and fastidiously. She could see the paint job had been done with great care and neatness; there were no splotches or drip marks anywhere. The transparent cupolas comprising the cockpit, gunner's turret and bomb bay were clear and clean, with no marks of glue at the edges. Evidently, he took great care of build quality, and she liked that. She hated slipshod, untidy work. Brijesh was totally focused on the job at hand and had seemingly even forgotten she was across the table from him. He was a perfectionist. Like those who had made Sohan Uncle's cameras and lenses. She liked watching such people work – the way they became totally immersed in what they were doing and were finicky about every detail. Fascinated, she watched him quietly for a good 20 minutes, appreciating the way his long fingers moved and worked.

Suddenly, he grunted in frustration. He'd been trying to install a minuscule silver screw into a slot with a jeweller's screwdriver, but the whole plane shifted and moved about when he did.

'Could you hold the plane still, please, while I screw this in?' he asked, glancing at her. She was standing at the side of the table, bent over like he was, her eyes fixed on the screw he had been trying to put in. Her flimsy pajama top hung loose on her slim shoulders and he could see right down her front as she bent over. He prised his eyes away, the heat rushing to his face.

'Oops!' she squeaked, blushing and straightening up and adjusting her top. 'Sorry! Okay!' She held the plane steady as he slotted in the screw.

'Thanks!'

'You take great care with your work!'

'You have to, otherwise what's the point?'

'How long has this taken you to make?'

'About three weeks to a month: I used to build it in the hospital where mom was.'

'Oh.'

He rubbed his eyes tiredly. 'Let's take a break,' he said, going to the bed. 'Hey, Djinn!' The big dog opened one rueful eye and sighed.

Shoma sat down on the bed beside him. 'Oh ya,' she said chirpily, 'I nearly forgot why I came here! About tomorrow morning …'

She talked volubly for five minutes, outlining her plan of action. He grinned.

'It should work!'

He went back to work after ten minutes and she watched him, mesmerized, until it was midnight. Occasionally, he asked for her assistance.

'I think we're done for the day,' he said at last, standing back. The plane squatted resplendently in the golden light of the goose-necked lamp. 'I just have to charge up the batteries and we'll be ready for testing.'

It warmed her from the inside – the way he had begun saying 'we' as if this had been a joint endeavour.

'Oh, one last thing before we shut shop!' he said now, 'Can you put these decal transfers on? I always make a mess of doing them.'

One by one, he took the decals and identification numerals off their backing, put them on a fingertip and handed them over to her.

'That one goes there! Great!' She put them on perfectly.

She had just taken the last two decals from his fingertips and was about to stick one of them on, at the spot he indicated on the fuselage, when the power went off. The room was plunged into darkness. Djinn raised his head and rumbled softly.

'Oh shit!'

'Don't move!' he said, 'I'll get my torch! It should be somewhere here!' He fumbled around cautiously, careful not to disturb the plane. 'Crap! It's not here!'

'There should be candles and a lantern on the sideboard behind me,' Shoma said. 'Nani keeps them in every room.'

'Oh …' He was still fumbling around. 'Can you get them?'

'I guess. But I've got two decals stuck to my fingers!' She paused. 'Okay, here's the thing. You come towards me. I'm holding out my other hand. I'll lead you to the sideboard and you'll find the candle and matches.'

'Okay,' he said doubtfully. He stretched out both arms, stepping away from the table. With the decal hand raised high, fingers well out of the way, Shoma stretched out her other arm and took a couple of steps forwards.

'Here!' she called softly. It was pitch black and she could see nothing. 'I'm right here!'

'Okay,' he grunted, taking another step forwards, and suddenly bumped into her. He found her searching hand and gripped it.

She turned around and led him to the sideboard, stepping very cautiously indeed. She felt around the sideboard and her hand closed over the candlestick. A box of matches lay alongside.

'Here,' she said, 'I've got them in my hand, matches and candle.' He felt her hand with both of his and took the candle from her.

'Got it, thanks!' The match flared and he lit the candle.

They went back to the worktable. 'Okay, you can stick those last two on,' he said, holding the candle well away from the table. He didn't want hot wax to fall all over his pristine plane. Carefully she bent forwards, tongue peeping out of her mouth, and placed the two last decals in their respective spots.

'There! All done!' she said, straightening up. 'It looks great!'

He stared at her. In the wavering golden candlelight, she looked utterly lovely, he thought. He walked past her and put the candle-stand back on the sideboard and went and stood beside her.

'It looks good,' he agreed, 'I hope it flies as well too!'

'Bet it will. You took such care! Your mom would have been so proud!'

He turned to her. 'I guess. This was the most difficult model I've built. When mom bought it, I thought it would be too complicated. But she said, "Just read the instructions and if you get stuck, ask me! I'm an engineer too!"'

Shoma felt the tears flood her eyes. 'I wish I could have met your mom,' she said softly. 'She sounds like a fabulous person!'

'I used to fight with her like anything,' he said, staring at the plane. 'I wanted us to leave papa but she wouldn't.'

'But why?'

'She said he was a sick person and that you didn't desert sick people but tried to take care of them so they got better. Can you imagine? She said that if we didn't look after papa he would end up roaming about in the streets and sleeping in the gutter and getting into trouble with the police, and we couldn't have that, could we?'

'Didn't your papa have a job?'

'Not for two years: he got chucked out for being drunk on his last job.'

'Your mom should have put him into one of those special hospitals they have for drunks. You know – where they treat them!'

'She did three times and he escaped all three times and came back home even worse!' He gulped. 'And then he used to beat her up!' He shut his eyes, his Adam's apple wobbling. 'The last … the last time …' he was almost whispering now, 'I was at home and … and instead of trying to help her I went and hid in my closet. I … I should have hit him with my cricket bat but I just let him beat her … he'd pushed her into my room and was beating her right there. I could have saved her but didn't! I could hardly face her after that … and never told her that I'd been in the closet. And then she fell ill soon afterwards and never came back from the hospital!' He was weeping openly now, 'But by then, in the end she did tell him to leave: he'd started hitting me too and she couldn't take that. So, he did end up roaming the streets and sleeping in the gutter. And then he heard that she had died and came back home and went totally berserk like some crazy elephant …'

He was weeping and trembling now, making tears flood her eyes again. Unhesitatingly, she took him into her arms, held him close and put up her face to his and kissed him on the lips. She hoped she had got it right because she had never kissed anyone on the lips before. Then her arms went around his waist and she just held him for minutes on end, trying to smother the sobs that had begun to wrack him and that terrifying trembling and to hold down her own sobs at the same time.

'Please don't cry,' she whispered, 'you're making me cry too – it upsets me too much!' For long moments, she held him as closely as she could and pressed her face against his cheek, kissing away the salty tears that ran down them, waiting for the trembling to subside. At last he calmed down and she stepped back, as he stared at her blearily and wiped his eyes. 'I'd better go now,' she whispered, also wiping her eyes and straightening her top again, 'see you early morning!'

Dumbly, he nodded.

Outside, another steady, heavy downpour thundered down incessantly. He climbed into bed, and slowly ran his tongue over his lips and felt his cheek where she had pressed her little nose and soft lips to it and thought about what Kusum had said because his heart was suddenly incandescent …

The diehard birders were up and about at 5.30 the next morning, gathering up their equipment and demanding tea.

'Kusum, keep breakfast ready for us by nine sharp!' Vinita Aunty ordered. 'We have to leave for the meeting immediately afterwards.'

'I just hope I can get some good recordings this morning,' Siddharth said.

'Kalpana, come with me. Let's see if Brijesh will come along with us today. He must have had enough of Shoma by now!' Aditi got to her feet.

But Brijesh's door was ajar. Tentatively they peeped in. The bed was made and the room was empty.

'He's not here! His bed hasn't been slept in!'

Kalpana looked shocked and pointed at Shoma's door. 'You mean … oh, my God, no! They wouldn't dare!'

'What do you expect?' Aditi said viciously, rolling her eyes at Shoma's firmly shut door.

'Should we?' Kalpana dared to ask.

Aditi shook her head. 'Sometimes,' she said, 'knowledge is power! We'll tell mama! Then the fat will really be in the fire!'

But, when they paused by the door and put their ears to it, they didn't hear a sound.

7

A little later that morning, the birders walked down along the lake path and then veered off up along the path leading up to the ridge and along the stream. They walked slowly, their ears pricked, eyes peeled, whipping up their binoculars every now and then. The morning chorus had just got going, and there was a cacophony of birdsong and calls emerging from the canopy and undergrowth. The heavy downpour through the night had made the ground soggy and saturated and they had to tread carefully, if squelchily. The clouds had drifted away now, leaving blue skies behind.

'Come on, you grey-winged blackbird, you're here somewhere, I know it!' Siddharth said importantly, trying to get beside Bony Mouse.

'That Shoma is so stupid,' Aditi exclaimed. Then she smiled. 'But we got her good, didn't we? Apart from the jailbreak, we know what's going on between her and that Brijesh!'

'Don't mention it,' Bony Mouse grinned. 'You should have seen her face when she opened the door and saw us all standing there like a welcome committee! It was priceless.'

'Shh … kids, keep it down!' Professor Damodar chided them.

'Hey, did you hear that?' Aditi exclaimed suddenly, a few minutes later, cocking her head and quickly switching on her mike.

Siddharth and Bony Mouse had fallen back and seemed to be chatting rather than listening. The adults were trailing even further back.

'What?' Zit-face asked.

'Don't really know … Hey, there it is again!' Now they could both hear a low but clear and sweet song, starting off with a long plaintive whistle that suddenly perked up cheerily, repeated three times and then lapsed back into silence.

'Wow! What on earth was that?'

'Don't know – go fetch Siddharth and papa and mama!'

'What is it?' Siddharth asked his sister a trifle irritably as she put her fingers on her lips.

'Shh … listen …' she indicated the direction in which the last call had come and Siddharth pointed his mike towards it, still frowning.

And then, from a slightly different location, the call came again! Both Aditi and Siddharth swung their mikes around excitedly. The bird seemed to be waiting for pauses in the dawn chorus before whistling. Bony Mouse and Zit-face were raking the foliage with their binoculars, trying to catch a glimpse of the elusive songster.

'There!' Aditi exclaimed suddenly, pointing as the adults shambled up to them.

Alas, it was just a yellowing leaf fluttering in an eddy of breeze.

'What is it, dears?' Meatloaf asked.

'Don't know, Aunty, but it sings beautifully! Papa, be ready with your camera: it might call again!'

'What is it?' Sohan Uncle asked.

'Can't quite make out – but I've got a good recording, papa,' Aditi said.

'So have I,' Siddharth added quickly.

He couldn't help feeling envious that Aditi had been the first to hear and record it.

'There it goes again!' Zit-face exclaimed as the lovely birdsong tinkled out of the forest.

The bird sang intermittently for about five minutes; it seemed to be moving around between snatches of song. They scanned the foliage again but never caught sight of it at all. In desperation, Sohan Uncle reeled off several shots of the foliage in the hope that when the pictures were scrutinized, the bird would show up in them. Then the bird fell silent.

'It's probably flown,' Siddharth said. 'Dammit, we didn't even catch a glimpse of it!'

'But we've got a good recording. Maybe we can play it at the seminar and someone will be able to identify it!' Professor Damodar said.

'Brilliant idea, uncle!' Siddharth said in his usual pompous manner.

They went back to the house for breakfast.

'Who heard it first?' Professor Damodar asked as they sat down.

'I did,' Aditi said proudly. 'I made the first recording.'

'Wonderful, my dear! Then if it is something new, you'll get the major credit for the discovery. If it's some new species, they'll have to name it after you!'

Aditi bridled, and Siddharth kicked himself under the table. If he had flirted less and listened more, he would have surely heard it first …

The door banged and Shoma and Brijesh entered; their cheeks pink, their eyes bright, hair tousled, Djinn padding beside them.

'Wow!' Shoma exclaimed. 'Riding a bike full tilt downhill first thing in the morning is really great! What's for breakfast? We're famished!' She looked around the table. 'Hi,' she said cheerfully, 'good morning everyone!'

The gang of four glanced at her in derision and turned their attention back to the recorder. Vinita Aunty looked like she had swallowed something vile.

'Play the call again, Siddharth,' Sohan Uncle said, 'let's listen to it carefully!'

'Here goes, papa!' He played the sweet song again.

'Any guesses?' Sohan Uncle asked the gathering.

'Could be a thrush of some kind,' Professor Damodar suggested.

'Sounds like a cross between an oriole and a shama,' Sohan Uncle said.

Shoma leaned forward, with her head cocked to one side, listening keenly.

'Why are you listening to it?' Aditi inquired sarcastically. 'It's a bird, after all!'

'I might not know what bird it is, but I could tell you if I've heard the song before,' Shoma replied sweetly. She shrugged nonchalantly and stared meaningfully at Aditi. 'After all, I live here, you know!'

'Yeah, yeah ...' Aditi muttered under her breath. 'Deaf as a post and blind as a bat though you may be!'

'What?'

'Nothing! We're not supposed to talk to you.'

'Why are you, then?'

'I'm not!'

'You just did. Everyone heard you.' Shoma raised her eyebrows. 'Unless they're all suddenly deaf as posts and also blind as bats as you all were when Aditi deliberately spilled Coke all over my painting!' She smiled blithely at the others. 'Three blind mice, see how they run ...' she sang.

Taken aback, Siddharth quickly played the recording again.

'Wow, it really sounds beautiful, doesn't it, Bridge? It sounds so sad at first and then happy,' Shoma said.

'Have you heard it before?' Brijesh asked sotto voce.

Shoma shook her head. 'No, I haven't. It must be really rare! Where did you guys hear it?'

'Down by the stream!' Siddharth blurted out before he clamped his mouth shut. 'Sorry, ma,' he said.

Meatloaf, who had still been nursing her grudge over the little brown bird, suddenly leaned forward. 'Shoma dear, isn't it time you apologized so we could all get back to normal again and everyone can talk to everyone? I'm sure Vinita Aunty will forgive you if you say sorry to Aditi and the others.'

'Sorry about what?' Shoma asked innocently.

'Charu, there's no point even trying,' Vinita Aunty said.

'Papa, we'll take a shot at it tomorrow morning again, okay?' Siddharth said. Sohan Uncle nodded.

'Yes. It should probably be there. This is the breeding season for most species so it must be marking its territory. Hopefully we'll get a recording and a visual.'

'Maybe it's a species that hasn't been discovered!' Bony Mouse said excitedly.

'You know what we'll do?' Sohan Uncle said. 'We'll play this recording at the site. If the bird is around, it'll turn up to check on who the interloper is. We're sure to get a visual that way.'

The birding group left to attend the seminar immediately after breakfast. Aditi tried desperately to rope in Brijesh, but he politely refused.

'Wow!' Shoma said as she watched them ride off on the donkeys. 'It's so nice to have the house to ourselves! What should we do? You know, I have school in two days' time ... just for a few days before the holidays begin. I really don't know why our holidays didn't start right after the exams!'

In the end, they decided to ride their bikes right around the lake. Kusum packed them some aloo paranthas and mango pickle.

'*Sambhal kar jaana!* Be careful,' she said smiling.

'Kusum Didi, don't worry, Djinn will be with us!'

Shoma waited till Kusum had left the room. 'Okay,' she said, 'we'd better take a couple of towels. We could get a bit wet!' She pulled out a couple of dark blue towels from the store-cupboard as he watched.

'You want another swimming lesson?' he asked.

'Nah, but there are streams we have to cross, and they must be pretty full after all the rain we've had.'

They rattled off on their bikes, Djinn by their side. The track hugged the lake, occasionally winding a bit inland. It was smooth in places, rather pebbly and rocky in others and often slushy. The streams that they had to cross rushed down the steep slopes, full pelt, reinforced by the recent rains. Shoma and Brijesh simply took off their jeans and waded across in their shorts, grinning foolishly at each other.

'I can't stand clammy jeans!' Shoma said as she stuffed them into her backpack, before they went across. 'And the water is pretty high!'

'These must be impossible to cross during the monsoons,' Brijesh remarked. 'The current is pretty strong already.'

'Yeah! Come along, we have a little more way to go before we come to the edge of the golf course. There's a big waterfall we have to get across but I've found a secret way through!'

As they approached the eastern end of the lake, they could hear the waterfall pounding down in a churn of white water.

'Okay,' Shoma said, 'we have to leave the bikes in their shelter and climb up along the waterfall.'

'Shelter? What do you mean?'

'Just follow me!' she said, grinning. She wended her way inland for a bit and then stopped near the base of a sheer cliff across a tumble of rocks. She walked behind a huge boulder that leaned against the cliff face … and disappeared. He followed and saw an opening in the cliff face, like a doorway. Shoma entered and indicated that he should follow her. There was a short narrow passage which turned sharply left almost immediately, widening slightly. Shoma flicked on her lighter and he saw an alcove sunk in the rocky wall to the left, with signs that someone had recently made a fire here.

'Come on,' Shoma said, 'the cave itself is just ahead.' It was a small cave, rather like a walk-in closet.

'This is where I leave the bike,' she said. 'Djinn and I found this place. Isn't it cool?'

'It's like those miniature Japanese hotel rooms they have at airports,' Brijesh said, standing beside her. He pointed to the alcove. 'Hey, look, someone's made a fire here!'

She grinned at him. 'I did, the last time I came here. It had started raining and gotten cold. I usually sit here with Djinn if it's raining or leave my bike here if I want to explore the waterfalls on foot. The best part is that the smoke from a fire goes straight out, so you don't cough or anything! I've even stored a garbage bag full of pine needles, pine cones, dry moss and firewood and matches to light another fire if needed. No point trying to collect wood and stuff when it's raining. I also brought some old cushions from the house so it's comfortable to sit and lie down. Anyway, we can park our bikes here and go on.'

He was impressed. Sure enough, right at the back, in the cave-room proper, there was what appeared to be a large black garbage bag, bulging at the seams, and a fat green backpack.

'This backpack is also yours?' he asked.

'Yes! That's got the cushions and two towels, one for me and one for Djinn. We often need to dry ourselves off after paddling in the pool or getting wet in the rain. And an old pair of shorts and a T-shirt too!'

'Wow! You sure think of everything!' She smiled shyly and went red.

'Okay, now what?' he asked after the bikes had been pushed into the cave. They went back outside.

Grinning, she pointed upwards. 'You see that – where the waterfall gushes madly over that rocky overhang? Well, there's a ledge behind it that we can walk along to the other side. We'll get a bit damp with the spray, but not soaking wet or anything like that.'

'Wow!' Again, he was hugely impressed. 'You really know this place like the back of your hand!'

Carefully, they climbed up along the falls. Huge glistening ferns, vines and epiphytes burgeoned everywhere.

'Okay,' she said, taking his hand. 'Here we go! We just have to step over this gap. Come on, Djinn!'

It was astonishing, standing behind the waterfall, which was like a silvery-bluish white veil in front of them.

'Wow!' he said, 'this is amazing!'

They crossed over. Bushes and trees climbed up the slope, marking the edge of the golf course. But it was crumbly and moist as a fruitcake here, and most of the trees had their roots exposed. Hand in hand, they emerged out of the trees, staring at the vast immaculate sward of green ahead.

'Come on, let's go on ahead.' Shoma's eyes danced with excitement. 'There's a deserted little shack just ahead. I think it was built for protection against the rain or something. We can eat there! Besides, it's beginning to drizzle.'

'Aren't we trespassing?' he asked.

'Well,' she said, arms akimbo, 'Nani said that Mr. Suraj Mukhi has trespassed and trampled all over the whole mountain!'

They slithered down the slope. Right next to the bordering trees was the little shack made of pine-logs.

Shoma stopped suddenly. 'What's that tall thing next to the shack?' she asked, frowning and pointing.

'It looks like a cage of some kind,' Brijesh said, puzzled, 'but it is empty!'

'Weird!'

It was, in fact, a cage mounted on wheels. It was about 10 feet tall, 8 feet long and 6 feet wide, with vertical iron bars and a drop-down door in its roof. Its roof was also wooden with a trapdoor at the top. The cage had been placed abutting the shack and facing the trees so that it was not visible from the golf course proper.

'Why the heck would anyone park a cage here?' Shoma asked, perplexed. Her brow cleared. 'Maybe they've seen a leopard or something and are planning to catch it? They were warning Nani about leopards and bears! Come on, let's get into the shack!'

They pushed open the creaking wooden door and went in. The shack seemed to have been a storage place for construction material originally, later upgraded to a rain shelter. It was furnished with three rickety wooden chairs, a wobbly table and an ancient wooden cupboard.

'You'll never guess what's in the cupboard!' Shoma said, grinning. 'The last time I came here, I opened it.'

'What?'

'There's a mouldy old golf bag with some rusty clubs, and some knives and forks and spoons and plates!'

There were two light sockets in the shack but with no bulbs in them. One small dirty window overlooked the lake.

They sat down at the table and opened the tiffin box Kusum had packed for them and tucked in hungrily. Big Djinn, of course, wolfed down his own fat rotis.

'He's a great dog!' Brijesh said, watching him. 'He's a cross between a German Shepherd and a Tibetan Mastiff, isn't he?'

'Ya – everyone said he'd be too ferocious to train, but you can see how good he is! He's not licky and slobbery like other dogs but he's fine!'

'Yes, he's so … so dignified! He doesn't fawn on anyone or try to climb into their laps like most dogs do.'

'Nani said you're going to be here for a month,' Shoma said, abruptly changing the subject.

'Yes …'

'And then you'll go back to Mumbai?'

'I guess!' His face closed down. It wasn't a prospect he wanted to think about.

'I'll miss you,' she said simply. 'I like you being here!'

He felt that incandescent wave of happiness flare up again.

'Thanks! I like being here too …' He smiled wryly, 'especially with all those nice bird-watchers!'

'Liar, liar, pants on fire!'

'I'll … I'll miss you too when I go back! And Big Djinn …'

'But in Mumbai you'll be staying with your dad?'

'I suppose,' he said dully. The prospect terrified him. 'I don't know how I'll manage alone. No help stays for more than a week … and he gets drunk every day and … and …'

'You don't have any other relatives to stay with?'

'No!'

He lapsed into silence, staring at the table.

'That's worse than mama and papa. They fight a lot but at least they bring me presents and I have Nani and Djinn!'

'I don't think papa even knows when my birthday is!' Brijesh said bitterly.

'I was very scared when I first came here to live,' she admitted. 'But Nani was really sweet and then found Djinn for me …'

He nodded. 'Mom used to talk about her all the time,' he said, 'she said she owed everything to her! You know, mom's mother died when she was very little and your Nani and Nana lived in the apartment next door, so your Nani sort of took over looking after mom. Your Nani taught in mom's school and encouraged her like anything. Even when mom went to college and IIT, your Nani told her to get her PhD and go abroad for further studies and research. She really mentored her all the way. Mom used to design rocket engines and satellites for ISRO, but she worked independently in Mumbai. They didn't like that very much but her designs and ideas were so brilliant, they just had to accept her work! She was talking to your Nani on the phone even when she was very, very sick and weak …'

'Ya, Nani said your mom was one of the most brilliant students she'd ever taught in forty years! But I never knew Nani sort of brought her up too!'

His eyes glimmered with tears again. 'Sorry!' he mumbled, 'I just think of mom so much!' She just nodded quietly and quickly wiped her own eyes. With an effort, he collected himself.

'I think we should head back – it's getting quite dark.' He looked out of the window.

'Oh crap! It looks like it's going to rain again!'

'It doesn't matter! We've got our raincoats this time!'

They made their way back up the slope, slipping and sliding in the slick mud.

'Just look at this stuff,' Brijesh remarked, 'it's all gooey and slippery and full of water like a muddy pudding!'

They went across the waterfall ledge and collected their bikes from the cave. A fine rain had begun to fall, gradually getting heavier. It was quite dark again by the time they reached the house.

'Kusum Didi!' Shoma yelled, 'Could you fry us some pakoras and samosas, please? We're famished!' Happily, they sat before the huge golden piles of piping hot pakoras and samosas that Kusum put before them. Shoma screwed up her face.

'You know, I have school day after. But what should we do tomorrow?'

'Can we go back to the island? I want to test out the plane.'

Her eyes gleamed. 'Sure! Great!' She leaned towards him and lowered her voice. 'But if those creeps want to go birding tomorrow morning we'll ...'

'Sure!' he grinned.

'Talk of the devils,' she said laconically as they heard the clop of donkeys' hooves on the tamped driveway outside, accompanied by argumentative voices. As usual, Vinita Aunty immediately demanded tea as Shoma smiled at her prettily.

'How was the seminar, Aunty?' she asked and got a glare in return. Oh yes, Vinita Aunty bore her grudges for a long time.

The birding group gathered at one end of the verandah, discussing the proceedings of the day. Shoma and Brijesh sat with Djinn at the other end and played Snap. But both of them were listening avidly to the birders' discussion.

Apparently, they had played the morning's recording to the participants and audience and it had generated considerable interest – and skepticism too. Some of the high-powered birders agreed it was an unusual call and song but they wouldn't accept the evidence without a visual.

'We'll have another shot at it tomorrow morning,' Sohan Uncle said. 'We'll play this recording where we heard it today and winkle out the fellow!'

'Oh my God, this is so exciting!' Aditi squealed.

Shoma arched her eyebrows at Brijesh and leaned over. 'Did you hear that?' Her eyes shone with mischief.

Nani called again that evening and was relieved to learn that there had been no further fireworks!

Meanwhile, a steady drumming on the roof signalled the start of another downpour. Luckily, yet again, it had cleared up by the morning, though it appeared to have rained through the night. The birding group set off at 6 a.m. Siddharth and Aditi were in a lather of excitement. Were they on the verge of discovering a new species? They were glad that their parents and Professor Damodar and Charulata Aunty had been with them when they had first heard and recorded the bird – it gave their claim full credibility.

When they arrived at the stream, Vinita Aunty and Meatloaf looked around warily, but there didn't seem to be any stinging insects around this morning. And then, amidst all the early morning bird cacophony, they heard the fluting call again.

'There – hear that!' Siddharth whispered, grabbing his father's elbow. His father raised his huge telephoto lens in the direction of the call and took a cautious step forward.

'It's staying in one place this time,' Aditi murmured. Meatloaf and Vinita Aunty, who had their backs to the sound, froze and very slowly twisted around, too afraid to move quickly. Professor Damodar, who had settled on a rock, lowered his binoculars and tried getting a fix on the exact spot from where the song emerged. Sohan Uncle took another step forward and then, in sheer desperation, reeled off a series of shots of the foliage. They could study the pictures minutely, and maybe winkle out the bird if it was hidden somewhere. But none of them had heard anything so beautiful before. He took another step forward and snapped a twig underfoot like a pistol shot.

Immediately, the birdsong stopped.

'It's gone. Sohan, you shouldn't have moved forward. It's obviously very shy!' Meatloaf was annoyed. 'Really, you photographers can't leave anything in peace; you have to try and get that one step closer and ruin everything for everyone!'

'We need a visual record!'

'At least we've recorded its song again,' Aditi said smugly. 'Twice in two mornings: that should count for something.'

'You know,' Professor Damodar suggested. 'You could play this at Siddharth's presentation at the seminar. Sir Harold Radcliffe should be there with other senior birders. He's an expert on birdsong and calls. He's sure to be able to identify it.'

Siddharth nodded eagerly. 'Yes, we could do it after my slide show!' The bird might be Aditi's find but the presentation was his!

They waited for another twenty minutes but there was no further song.

'Okay, kids, let's go back to the house – it looks like it's going to rain again,' Sohan Uncle said.

At the house, they found Shoma and Brijesh at the dining table wolfing down their breakfast.

'Good morning!' Shoma greeted the birding party cheerfully, her eyes sparkling as Brijesh quietly ate his mushroom omelette. 'How many species did you knock off this morning?'

'Brijesh, you really should have come with us,' Aditi said, ignoring Shoma, 'we heard that mystery bird again this morning. I was the first to hear it yesterday! We've got more recordings, which we're going to play at the seminar during Siddharth's presentation. You must come for that! We wanted to take you along this morning but you weren't in your room!' She looked meaningfully at Shoma.

'We'd gone for a walk with Djinn!' Brijesh said. 'It had stopped raining at last.'

'And what are you doing today?' Aditi asked, never one to give up easily.

'I have to test fly my plane,' Brijesh answered truthfully. 'It's almost done!'

'Oh … can't you do that some other time?'

'No, the weather's cleared – it'll be good for flying.'

'Too bad!'

Vinita Aunty frowned. 'This plane of yours, Brijesh … it has an engine?'

He nodded. 'Four motors actually,' he said proudly. 'It's a Lancaster bomber!'

'I hope it doesn't make that irritating buzzing noise that most model planes make; they disturb the birds for miles around.'

'Aunty, the birds get used to it. In Mumbai, sometimes the kites even try to attack the models!'

'Whatever it is, it is a disturbance and if it crashes into a bird, it will kill or injure it!'

'I won't crash it into any bird,' Brijesh said. 'And it doesn't make all that much noise. Like a chainsaw does!'

'And like I suppose Mr Suraj Mukhi's fancy resort and golf course has done,' Shoma butted in, unable as usual to hold her tongue. 'He cut down so many trees and flattened that mountaintop so that grown men could hit a small ball into a hole! God knows how many animals and birds he killed and injured doing that!' She got a black look from the adults and shrugged. 'It's true!'

Thankfully, the birders left for their seminar right after breakfast.

'*Rubadubdub*, three nuts in a tub!' Shoma sang cheerfully as she, Brijesh and Djinn got into the boat a little while later. Djinn sat at the prow as usual and the beautiful Lancaster bomber and its control panel occupied the middle seat, lightly fastened with twine. Brijesh was happy to sit alongside Shoma at the stern.

'I hope it flies,' he said nervously, 'I always get a bit panicky before the first flight.'

'It should. You've charged the batteries to bursting and tested the engines at home too.'

'I guess. If it flies well today, I'll fit the two mini-cameras tomorrow: one in the cockpit and the other in the bomb bay. They'll shoot video and pictures.'

'Wow!'

They made their way up to the grassy knoll. Brijesh felt the grass. It was smooth and soft and short – perfect for a runway. He set up his equipment and checked the direction of the wind.

'Okay, Shoma, now just hold her while I check the engines.'

Gently, she held the plane, and watched him.

'Motor 1 starting up!' The propeller spun as the motor buzzed to life.

'Motor 2, motor 3, motor 4!' The buzzing increased in intensity and Shoma could feel the plane shudder gently beneath her hands.

'It wants to take off!' she said. 'It wants to be free!'

'Check ailerons, rudder – both responding well! We're ready for take-off!' He grinned at her. 'Okay, let her go!' She let go and knelt back on the grass, watching in astonishment. The plane trundled across the grass, bobbing and swaying just a bit, gaining speed – and suddenly it was airborne. Brijesh stood with the control panel in his hand, juggling the control toggles.

'Wow!' she said, 'this is so cool!' The plane soared and banked like a bird, gaining height over the lake. She picked up her binoculars and followed it.

'She's a little nose-heavy,' Brijesh remarked, 'she needs more power to keep her nose up and flying. She'll use up more power!'

'How much battery life do you have left?'

He checked the panel. 'Oh, still about 10 to 12 minutes.'

'She's right over the lake. You'd better bring her back over the island. You don't want her to ditch in the water!'

He grinned.

'Come here,' he said, 'Wanna learn how to fly?'

Delightedly, she nodded.

'Okay,' he said, 'Check out the panel. This controls the rudder which will make her turn left or right; these four are the engine power controls; these control the flaps which make her lift or lose height and slow down, you can make her bank left like this, and right like that, but watch your airspeed then, because if you get too slow she'll roll over and go into a spinning dive and crash ...'

She looked at him, bemused. 'Slow down, slow down!'

'Okay,' he said gently taking her hand and placing it on the rudder control. 'Move it left, gently, and watch the plane ...' She felt his fingers move and watched the plane beginning to turn.

'Wow!' she breathed, gazing at the buzzing speck high up.

'Now we straighten up and turn the other way!'

'*Bridge, watch out – the bird is after it!*'

In a second he saw the peril. In their involvement with flying the Lancaster they hadn't noticed a peregrine take off from its rocky ledge and climb into the sky. Now it was diving straight at the plane, screaming down towards it at 320 kilometres per hour!

'Take the controls!' Shoma screamed as Brijesh grabbed them from her. With steely concentration, he watched the falcon swoop towards his beautiful plane. Both would be irrevocably damaged if the bird hit the plane. At the last moment, Brijesh banked the plane away from the meteor-like bird and put her into a screaming dive. The bird missed, looked surprised, gained height and scanned the sky. His face set, Brijesh pulled the Lancaster out of its dive perhaps just 20 feet above the lake, and made her climb again.

'Where's the bird?' he asked, his eyes on the plane.

'It's circling high up again,' Shoma said, squinting up into the sky. 'It's flying in front of the sun!'

The Lancaster rose above the island and Brijesh guided it down back to its grassy knoll runway.

'Whew!' he said relieved, 'I don't want to get into a dogfight with that thing!' But he was hugely excited too. Flying a remote-control plane was fun, but flying it in the presence of a bird that thought it to be a kill, was something else – a real life dogfight! Once he fitted the cameras on to the plane, he'd be able to get fair warning of the bird's approach and take evasive action accordingly. Of course, his plane didn't have any form of self-defense, which in a way was a pity, but he didn't want to harm the bird either. For both his plane's sake and the bird's survival, he just had to ensure that his flying skills were good enough to prevent the disaster.

Game on!

'Wow!' Shoma breathed. 'That was some escape!'

'Thanks for spotting it,' he said. 'Otherwise both the plane and the bird would have been in the lake!'

'Thanks for trying to teach me to fly!'

He grinned. 'You know what would be really fun?'

'What?'

'If we both had fighters armed with functioning paint guns. I believe you can get them: they actually fire little pellets filled with paint like a machine-gun so you can have dogfights. When you land back on the ground, you check which plane has been hit more times.'

The wind had freshened up again and the sun had become hazy.

'Uh-oh,' Shoma exclaimed pointing towards the high mountains, 'Looks like we're going to get another load of rain! It's really rained so much these last few days and the monsoons haven't even set in properly. I tell you, the weather is going haywire!'

'Let's go back. I don't want the plane and control panel to get wet!'

'Come on, Djinn!'

In the afternoon, Shoma watched Brijesh install and test the two tiny cameras on the plane. It had started raining again and gotten cold and she had asked Kusum to light a fire in his room.

'Where did you get these cameras from?' she asked.

'Mom bought them for me,' he said, 'she said they're not very expensive so it won't matter too much if they get totalled in a crash. But they're surprisingly good and have very sharp wide-angle lenses.'

He installed one camera in the plane's cockpit canopy and the other in the gunner's turret below.

'Pity we can't test these now,' she said. She frowned. 'What are you going to do tomorrow? I have school. I bet that Aditi will try and drag you to that seminar.'

'If the weather is clear, I thought I might go back to the island and test out the plane's cameras in flight,' he said. 'That's if you don't mind me taking *Rubadubdub*!'

'Sure, you can take *Rubadubdub*! And you know what? I'll leave Djinn behind with you too: then Aditi won't dare come anywhere near you!'

'Thanks,' he grinned.

'You'd better watch out for that bird!'

'Well, I'll have two eyes in the sky on board the plane!'

If the bird did attack, he thought, this time he would not flee! He would dodge and dart till it tired and gave up! Sure, the Lancaster was a relatively cumbersome plane compared to say a Spitfire or Hurricane, but still. No bird ought to make it turn tail and flee!

8

Yet again, it had rained heavily all night and continued in the early morning, ruining the birders' plan to check out the mystery bird once more. The rain seemed to have become a pattern. But by 8 a.m. or so, the clouds had begun to disperse, though it was now too late for the bird-watching group to go in search of their elusive songster – they had to leave for the seminar by 8.30 a.m. at the latest. But they were excited: two world-renowned bird-watchers, Sir Harold Radcliffe and Dr. Premlata Pushkarna, were due to arrive that day and would stay at Cloud-house. Both were experts at identifying birdsong and calls.

'If it's clear tomorrow, we'll take them along,' Professor Damodar said. 'Hopefully, the mystery bird will still be around!'

Sure enough, Aditi had once again tried roping Brijesh into accompanying them to the seminar.

'I have to work on my plane and then test fly her!' he told her as if the nation's future depended on it.

'But it'll probably be raining …'

'I have to do some bench-tests,' he said, sounding as pompous as Siddharth and making Shoma choke back a giggle. 'Those are done indoors.'

'But what'll you do alone?' Aditi went on peevishly.

'Oh Aditi, don't worry, I'm leaving Djinn with him,' Shoma said sweetly. 'He won't be alone. But thank you for caring!'

Aditi made a face but thankfully shut up.

'I'll have to leave for school by 8 o'clock,' Shoma told Brijesh. 'Ride with me to the car park, and then you can bring Grumpy back so the others can take him.' All seven of the donkeys were at the back door, waiting to take the birders to the car park.

'Won't he mind two people on his back?' Brijesh asked, 'I can easily walk alongside!'

'Nah! He's very strong! He won't mind.' She whispered something to him and looked pointedly at Meatloaf. 'If he can take her without batting an eyelid, he can take four of us easily!'

'Give me your backpack,' he said, taking her bright yellow school backpack and slinging it over his own shoulders.

'Thanks!'

It was just lovely sitting behind her on the donkey, his hands gently around her waist as they trotted off, with Djinn by their side. She turned around and flashed him a smile of incredible sweetness.

'I'll be back by 4 or 4.30. Grumpy will be at the car park to bring me home.'

'I could come to fetch you too,' he said. She turned around and smiled at him.

'You're sweet!' she said, her lips brushing his cheek. He went scarlet.

From the kitchen window Kusum and Annie watched them clop away and exchanged amused glances.

'*Lagta hai, Shoma baby bhi usko bahut pasand karti hain! Yaha chhoti si romance ho rahi hain!* It looks like Shoma baby likes him very much too! A little romance has got going here!' Kusum said, smiling.

'He seems to be a decent boy, and according to madam he's been through a lot. Besides, he makes his own bed every morning.' Annie said. For her, anyone who did that had been brought up properly.

Shoma's school van turned up punctually at 8.30 a.m. and she waved madly to Brijesh, gently holding Djinn by the collar. The huge dog had understood straightaway that he was to remain behind with his new friend.

'Come on Djinn, let's go back!' Brijesh said.

They clopped up to the top of the ridge and were about to begin their descent towards the house when Djinn began growling. He stopped suddenly and sniffed the air, his tail up, a low malevolent rumble rising from his throat.

'What's the matter, boy?' Brijesh reined in the donkey and looked around. The ridge top seemed deserted as it normally was. The two narrow paths leading off from the ridge wound their way through the pines and deodars. The path to the left, he knew, led to a deep gully or crevasse while the one

on his right wound its way to another gully, which led to
the place where he and Shoma had stopped and admired the
view when she had first taken him out. He was unaware of
a third thin trail leading off northwards, right down to the
lake – quite near the house, in fact. The trail meandered
parallel to the lake and emerged again at the lake's edge, very
near where Shoma usually moored *Rubadubdub*.

Brijesh looked around warily. There were leopards and
bears in these forests and mountains. Had Djinn just smelt
one? Nose down, Djinn had taken the path leading off to the
right and followed it for a bit, still rumbling. He stopped at
the turnoff, looked intently down the path and then trotted
back to Brijesh, giving him a baleful look and a perfunctory
lick on the hand that seemed to signal 'all clear, let's go, but
watch your back, boy!'.

'Come on, Grumpy, let's go!' Brijesh said, urging on his
steed. The donkey shuffled forward as the big dog kept pace
by his side.

Brijesh had wanted to go to the island as soon as possible,
but the weather played hide and seek with him all morning.
It would clear up brilliantly for a while, and then suddenly a
flotilla of thunderclouds would sail over again.

Then at last, at about 2.30 p.m., it seemed to clear
properly. Brijesh waited for fifteen minutes and then decided
to set off. He knew he would probably be too late to pick
up Shoma from school, but it couldn't be helped. He'd been
cooped up indoors all day and was fed up of it, and his plane
was in perfect condition to fly. He told Kusum he'd be taking

the boat out and set off. She smiled at him and quickly made him several fat chicken sandwiches.

'Thank you!' He put the box in his backpack, took a water bottle and checked all his equipment. He carried his basic model-making tools too, in case he needed to carry out running repairs, as well as a roll of cling-film in which to wrap the plane and its controls in case it started raining. Then he called Djinn and they set off, the dog also relieved to be going outdoors at last.

They set off in *Rubadubdub*, and suddenly he so wished Shoma was with him. But still, he'd fly the plane with the cameras working and show her the shots on his laptop later. This was only a trial flight anyway. He reached the island around 3.40 p.m. and began the climb to the top. Had he been at the top at that time, and looked over the lake, he would have seen the blue and white speedboat leave the resort dock and head swiftly across the lake to its southern shore.

He reached the top ten minutes later and began setting up his equipment. The breeze was fairly brisk and he knew the plane would have to fight strong headwinds during her flight. Also, more worryingly, it was beginning to get cloudy again. For a moment, he wondered if he should abandon the flight. But well, now that he was here, he could have her up and flying in five minutes and bring her down at the first sign of rain.

'Okay, Djinn, now let's fly this thing and do some aerial photography, shall we?'

He set up the cameras and checked that they worked.

'Okay boy, here goes! Fingers crossed!'

He set the plane on the runway as Djinn watched interestedly.

The Lancaster bomber took off into the ivory skies – very similar to the kind of skies the actual bombers had taken off in, nearly 80 years ago, to bomb German towns.

'Okay,' he said, 'Camera 1, let's have you!' Camera 1 was the one mounted on the gunner's turret.

'Oh, wow!' Camera 1 was transmitting live to his laptop.

'Camera 2, now ...' He switched to the second camera's transmission. Perfect!

'Great, now let's go!' He switched back to Camera 1 and switched on the engines. He watched, transfixed, out of the corner of his eye as he got a view of the take-off from the belly of the plane – the bumpy, shaky take-off, tufts of grass bending over as the plane trundled over them, and then the sky appearing suddenly as the plane lifted off. His other eye was on the control panel, feeding in the power and ensuring the plane lifted up levelly. He levelled her off and then switched to Camera 2.

'Wow, this is just so cool!'

Excited beyond measure, he flew the plane across the lake, glancing at his laptop that was receiving images transmitted by the cameras. They were taking breathtaking shots of the view from above, of the dark blue lake and the surrounding mountains and forest.

He banked her northwards, heading towards the golf course. And, too late, spotted the falcon again, already whistling down, talons extended. It hit the fuselage of the plane with its talons, sending it into a spiralling dive.

'Mayday! Mayday! Mayday!' Brijesh yelled automatically, as his laptop monitor showed terrifying footage of a plane in uncontrolled freefall heading straight for the water. The shock of impact seemed to have made the motors cut out and Brijesh toggled the switches desperately. He breathed a sigh of relief as he heard the faraway buzz and saw that the propellers had started whirring again. Thank God, all the antennae were still receiving and transmitting signals. The falcon, too, had received a nasty surprise: it hadn't expected to hit something so solid and was now circling high just watching again, reluctant to press home its attack. His face set, Brijesh yanked back the controls, giving her full power as she went into a spearing nosedive and then desperately pulled up the nose. She levelled out just metres from the water and began to climb steeply again. But, within seconds, Brijesh knew his beautiful Lancaster wouldn't be able to fly all the way back to the island. She had obviously suffered some severe damage, because she was juddering massively, her aerodynamic stability completely out of kilter. He would have to ditch her in the lake … Or else …

His face grim, he yanked the rudder, making the plane bank sharply. She lost height rapidly, but that was all right, because he was going to put her down. The golf course island loomed up in Camera 2. She was coming down too fast, so he reduced power as she skimmed over Green No. 10. And then she landed in a sand bunker, throwing up a welter of wet sand, and gently keeled over. She shuddered a bit and then the motors died and she lay still. The cameras went out.

'Oh crap!' Quickly, he packed up the control unit. 'Come on, Djinn, we have to go and retrieve her!' In his haste, he failed to notice the massive phalanx of indigo and gunmetal-coloured clouds smothering the high mountains at great speed. He did notice that the wind had suddenly picked up considerably, and was just grateful that the gusts had started after his beloved plane had landed. But now he had to get her.

He got into *Rubadubdub* with Djinn and set off. There was sure to be a landing jetty on the island to allow the golfers to get on to it. As he predicted, there was one on the side facing the main course and he bumped up to it gently, jumped across and fastened the boat.

'Come on, Djinn,' he said, heading for the stone steps that led up from the docks to the green above. It had suddenly grown dark and ominous and he snatched up the roll of cling-film he had brought just for such an occasion. Rain would short-circuit everything! He got to the top and looked around. Djinn ran on ahead and then stopped and looked back at him.

'She came down a little below the green in a bunker,' he muttered as Djinn disappeared into a bunker. Then Djinn emerged again and barked. 'Oh, you've found her? Good boy!'

He got down into the bunker and walked up to Djinn, who was now sitting beside his wreck. He knelt down beside the upside-down plane and looked at it, his heart thumping.

Carefully, he lifted it and inspected it. The damage didn't seem as bad as he had feared. The top of the fuselage had been raked open by the bird's talons: that had probably caused the turbulence, but it could be fixed. He'd have to check out the motors and other systems back in the house. He wrapped the cling-film around the plane and climbed out of the bunker. Then he noticed the blue and white speedboat churning swiftly across the lake from the southern shore, a man in a camouflage jacket at the tiller. Instinctively, Brijesh dropped down flat on the wet grass and focused his binoculars on the boat. Perhaps Shri Mukhiji had come to see Shoma's Nani again, not knowing she wasn't in. As Brijesh watched, another man emerged from the cabin, holding something in his hand. He put it down next to him and said something to the man at the tiller, making an exasperated face.

Brijesh stiffened and focused and refocused his binoculars, not quite believing what he was seeing. The second man had just brought out a backpack from the cabin. Then he looked around and picked up a pair of stout black leather shoes from the floor of the boat and stuffed them into the backpack.

It was a backpack Brijesh recognized immediately; as well as the shoes.

It was Shoma's bright yellow school backpack and those were Shoma's school shoes.

'What the …?' he muttered, mystified. Had something happened to Shoma? Had she had an accident on her way back from school? But why should these suspicious-looking fellows have gotten her backpack and shoes? Had they robbed, or worse, kidnapped her? But they were Suraj Mukhi's bodyguards ... he recognized the speedboat. It didn't make sense. Nothing made sense. He followed the speedboat through the binoculars as it approached the island, wondering if he had been spotted. But it skirted the island and made for the northern shore. He watched as it docked and the men tethered it. Then they both disappeared inside the cabin. A minute later they emerged, one of them carrying a bulky jute sack over his shoulder. The other man picked up the backpack and both began climbing the stone steps up towards the clubhouse. Oblivious of the deluge, now thundering down steadily, Brijesh made his way to the northern extreme of the island and focused on the clubhouse, into which the men had disappeared. The light was fading fast as the clouds loomed low, occasionally blotting out everything. But then a door on one side of the clubhouse opened and a beam of light speared out. A rather swanky blue and white golf cart drove out with one of the men at the wheel, the other sitting beside him. The jute sack was in the back. The headlamps of the golf cart made it easy to follow and he watched as it drove right across the course – straight towards the little wooden shack where he and Shoma had had their lunch the other day. The men parked the golf cart right next to the shack and got off. They lugged out the sack, which now appeared to have taken on a life of its own because it was wriggling. They thrust it into the shack along with the yellow backpack and then went in, slamming the door behind them. A light suddenly flared from the window as if a lantern had been lit.

Brijesh did not hesitate. 'Come on, Djinn, we have to go!'

Djinn watched him and whined. He knew something was bothering his new friend. Brijesh ran down the rain-slicked steps, clutching onto his precious plane and still not quite believing what he had seen. There could only be one thing—well, person—in that jute sack.

Shoma!

But why? Why the heck would someone as rich as Shri Suraj Mukhi want to kidnap Shoma? He had more than enough money! Brijesh got to *Rubadubdub* and sensibly began rowing the best he could. Someone would be sure to hear the outboard if he started her up. The oars splashed a bit and he grimaced, but luckily the rain would drown out any splashing sound. He rowed the boat past the gushing waterfall to a spot where he could perhaps moor the boat and continue on foot. It was a slushy, muddy section of the shore but he landed the boat and tied her up. Then he picked up his plane and began the slippery climb towards the waterfall. He stopped at the cave Shoma had shown him and left his plane and backpack inside.

'Okay, boy, now here we go!'

It was twilight dark and the rocks were treacherously slippery as he made his way up along the now roaring waterfall. He was soaked to the skin. He got to the ledge behind the waterfall and gasped as the cold water showered down on him. It was far more forceful than it had been the last time. He got across somehow and, ducking low, emerged at the edge of the golf course. He could see the dim shape of the shack now, with the light spilling out of its window. He held Djinn by the collar and approached, noticing that the ground was shaky and wobbly and unpleasantly squelchy underfoot, nearly causing him to lose his balance.

'Okay, boy, quiet, easy now! We'll check out the situation and then decide our plan of action!' He prayed the dog would keep quiet and not raise hell. Djinn might be formidable but there was nothing he could do against a hail of bullets. The dog whined anxiously.

'Okay, boy – down and stay!' Brijesh said quietly but firmly, wondering if Djinn had even been taught these commands. To his delighted surprise, the dog obeyed him immediately, hunkering down and watching him.

'Good boy!' Brijesh went into a commando crawl right up to the shack. Djinn stayed where he was. Brijesh crouched under the window, his heart thumping. The men's voice floated out.

'*Call aaya – usko pakda hain, laa rahe hain! Sahib khud laa rahain hain!* The call came, it's been caught and is being brought here: the sahib is bringing it here himself.'

What the heck did these men mean?

The answer became clear very quickly indeed. Above the sound of the rain hammering down, Brijesh heard the sound of a guttural diesel engine approaching. He peered around the shack and shrank back quickly. A big silver Isuzu pickup, with dazzling lights blazing, was driving across the golf course towards the shack, kicking up tufts of grass and clods of mud, its engine revving. Fastened down on its bed

183

was the cage that had been here the last time he and Shoma had come here. Only now, the cage was not empty.

Inside it, a furious but beautiful leopard paced round and round, snarling and growling. Brijesh ran back to Djinn, who remarkably was still obeying orders, though now growling deep in his throat, his lips drawn back over his gleaming canines.

He had smelt and heard the leopard all right. He knew this leopard. They had met before.

The pickup parked next to the golf cart. Two men jumped out, one of them holding open the door and unfurling an umbrella.

Shri Suraj Mukhi, complete with orange tilak and raw silk achkan, stepped out of the Isuzu pickup. The three men glanced at the snarling leopard and went into the shack, at the door of which the other two men stood, waiting.

What Brijesh overheard next chilled his blood. He crouched down by the window, one hand firmly gripping Djinn's collar. The dog was rumbling steadily now, balefully eyeing the leopard. Shri Suraj Mukhi was instructing his men in Hindi.

They would, when the rain let up a bit, take the little girl and drop her into the leopard's cage. The animal would do what it had to with her, after which they would tranquilize it with a dart. The remains of the girl and the leopard would then be taken back across the lake at night and thrown in the gully near the ridge. The leopard would probably recover and wander off, or help itself to the girl. Her remains would be found the next day, surely, and the old buddhi would have got her just deserts. He had warned her that the forests around here could be dangerous for little girls ... Now would she agree to sell her property?

Poor Brijesh went all hot and cold and began trembling. He needed a plan – and fast! He closed his eyes.

Okay, the first order of the day was to get the leopard out of the way. Brijesh eyed the cage. The animal was now lying down, exhausted.

'Djinn, sit and stay!' Brijesh said firmly. The big dog whined anxiously and sat down, watching him. He'd picked up yet another familiar scent: that of his beloved mistress. She was somewhere nearby. But he trusted this boy too.

Brijesh flitted up to the Isuzu and opened the door. He climbed up onto the roof and walked over the top of the cage, praying that the leopard would not leap up and claw at him through the roof. The animal crouched down and snarled furiously, watching the roof. Brijesh staggered across the cage and then lifted the drop-down door at the end. The leopard was now free to go. But the wretched creature just crouched at the back of the cage, snarling.

'Flush him, Djinn!' Brijesh said urgently. The big dog needed no second bidding. The leopard spotted him at once and fled out of the cage like a bolt of gold – he knew this enemy too! With a deep-throated bark, Djinn went after him as Brijesh leapt down and ducked behind the shack. Within seconds the men were at the door, shouting in alarm.

'*Bhaag gaya!* It's run away!' Three of them rather foolishly went on foot in pursuit of the leopard, which was now streaking across the golf course with the huge dog behind it. Shri Mukhi and the remaining man shut the shack door, ran to the Isuzu and started it up. Brijesh watched it lurch away at top speed. Shri Mukhiji himself was now in the passenger seat, pointing a rifle out of the window.

Brijesh rushed inside the shack. There in one corner was the wriggling sack, securely tied up with jute rope at the neck, the yellow backpack beside it.

'Budgie, are you all right?' he yelled, his cold wet fingers making a hash of untying the knots. The sack wriggled weakly. Brijesh dashed to the rickety wooden cupboard and yanked it open, snatching up a table knife, even as the mouldy old golf bag with its rusty clubs tumbled out at his feet. With gritted teeth, he sawed at the rope and at last it gave. Within seconds, he had pulled out a white-faced Shoma. She was gagged and bound, her eyes rolling wildly, her once pristine school uniform muddy and heavy with water. Her ankles and thighs were bound tightly, as were her delicate wrists. Somehow, he undid her knots without cutting her and put his arms around her, appalled as he felt her body shivering violently.

'Come on, let's get out of here!' He slung on her backpack and then took her hand and helped her stand, noticing that she was only in her socks and that her teeth were chattering.

'Wait!' he said, 'your shoes!' He pulled them out of her backpack and buckled them onto her shaking feet.

'There we are – let's go!'

'Br…Brij! Brij I c…can't feel my lll…legs at all. They had tied them so tightly!' She collapsed at his feet. While being taken from Grumpy, she had kicked one of the men in the face and he had furiously ripped off her shoes and tied her legs especially tight, both at the ankles and above her knees, to teach her a lesson.

Brijesh just picked her up in his arms and stood up. 'I've got you! Now let's go!'

'Wh…where's Djinn?' she asked.

'He's chasing the leopard!' He walked towards the door.

'Oh crap, they've come back!' The Isuzu pickup had returned. The leopard and dog had disappeared into the darkness, as had the three men on foot. Within seconds, Shri Suraj Mukhi and his unsavoury bodyguard were standing at the door, leering at them. The bodyguard now held the rifle, pointing it at them.

'*Hillo matt!* Don't move!'

Brijesh froze. Shri Suraj Mukhi whispered something to his bodyguard, who gave him the gun, then stepped forward and picked up a golf club, twirling it in his hands. Shri Suraj Mukhi took the club, putting the rifle on the table while the bodyguard pulled out another club for himself.

'Can you call Djinn?' Brijesh whispered to Shoma.

'Now, my friends, we are going to bash your heads in with this and throw you down a gully and roll rocks over you so everyone will think you died in a rock-fall!' Shri Mukhi said, furious that his original plan had been sabotaged.

Shoma quickly put two shaky fingers in her mouth and whistled like a football referee calling a foul. Outside, Djinn had given up the chase—the leopard had fled—and was galloping back to the shack when he heard his mistress's whistle.

'Get behind me!' Brijesh grunted, putting Shoma down. 'Hold onto me if you can't stand!' He had not been able to protect his mom. He would not make that mistake with Budgie. It would be impossible to live with such shame. It didn't seem that he would be able to save Budgie (let alone himself) once the golf clubs came whistling down, but at least he would not die a coward.

The man was grinning now, taking a step towards them and raising the club high. He was the same fellow Shoma had kicked in the face.

Just then, Shri Suraj Mukhi's phone began playing a religious tune. He put down the club and took the call.

'What?' he snapped. *'What?! The clubhouse is sliding towards the lake? Are you drunk?'*

For a second, the man with the golf club hesitated and watched his boss. From outside, over the rain, the children heard the deep angry baying of Djinn as he raced back.

'Djinn!' Brijesh yelled and poor Shoma stuttered as loud as she could, 'Kill him!'

Eighty kilos of furious muscle and power burst into the shack and slammed into the bodyguard from behind. He crashed down, knocking himself unconscious against the table edge. Already Shri Suraj Mukhi had turned to grab the rifle, but before he could reach it the dog was at his throat, snarling horribly. He screamed and desperately shook himself free and fled out of the door, but not before Djinn had ripped a gaping hole in the back of his churidar.

All this while, something very strange and frightening had begun to happen. Slowly, the floor of the shack had started tilting forwards, like a ship beginning to list prow-first into the sea. Cracks zig-zagged down the walls like bolts of black lightning.

'Can you walk?' Brijesh asked again, now barely able to keep his own balance. Shoma tried getting to her feet but collapsed. 'I ss...still can't feel anything in my legs,' she whispered. 'They're like wood!'

'Okay, whoops, what's happening? Earthquake – we'd better get out.' Again, he simply lifted her up and staggered out with her in his arms. The Isuzu pickup was driving very erratically towards the clubhouse, which was now tilting at an alarming angle and beginning to slide inexorably towards the edge of the cliff. The pickup looked as though it would tip over on to its side any moment. The whole golf course quivered and trembled as though someone had firmly tapped the top of a gigantic jelly.

Brijesh would never know from where he got the strength to scramble up the slippery muddy slope into the trees towards the waterfall ledge, holding Shoma in his arms. The ground beneath his feet seemed to be turning to liquid mud – it was like stepping into chocolate pudding. Shoma just clung on to him, her arms around his neck, her eyes wide with fright. Djinn followed them closely.

'We have to cross quickly,' Brijesh said over and over again. 'Wait a sec!' He put her down and then picked her up and lay her over his shoulder, in a fireman's lift. It was easier to keep his balance and hold Shoma this way. Thank God his mom had taught him this technique! The waterfall was roaring mightily now as he cautiously stepped his way across; the icy spray, almost as strong as from a fireman's hose, made them both gasp. Midway, he stopped, panting heavily.

'I'm going to put you down for a minute, to catch my breath! But I'm going to hold you up from under your arms!' Above the roar of the falls, they could hear a deep rumble. Djinn whined anxiously.

'My legs,' Shoma squeaked, 'I've got ttt-terrible cramps and ppp…pins and needles now!'

'Good!' he said, 'it means the circulation is coming back! They must have been tied very tightly.' Gamely, he picked her up again and made for the other end.

'I think I can just about manage now,' she said weakly as he laid her down after they had reached the other side. Djinn gave her face a quick lick. But then from across the waterfall there was a rumbling roar, the likes of which they had never heard before. It was a deep-throated angry sound, a malevolent, menacing growl and bellow from the very earth itself. It was nearly dark and still raining hard but through the trembling, shaking trees on the other side they saw something that made them cling together and whimper with fright.

Across the waterfall, the entire golf course appeared to be collapsing; slipping and sliding inexorably towards the cliff edge in a slow-moving gargantuan landslide. With a roar that sounded like the end of the world, it then tipped and slid right off the edge, huge dark cracks appearing on the grassy surface as it slid. Colossal chunks of earth and rock slid over the edge and smashed into the rocky ledge beneath where the fancy resort and Shri Suraj Mukhi's luxury villa had been built, followed by what seemed like the entire golf course. There was a sharp, loud crack like the sound of a lightning strike and the entire ledge teetered and collapsed into the lake first as if in slow-motion and then just tumbled down, taking the resort and villa with it. A wave of tumultuous brown and white water shot up angrily 15 to 20 feet high and surged across the lake in all directions at high speed.

'Oh, shit!' Shoma whispered. 'Nani had said he'd made the whole mm-mountain unstable!'

'Let's go to the cave. It seems safer on this side!'

'Yes,' she said simply, 'thank God they h…haven't cut any trees on this side!'

The now icy mountain winds and rain had still not finished with them. Drenched and chilled to the marrow, they stumbled into the cave and collapsed with relief, with Djinn snuggling down beside them. Both of them were shivering uncontrollably, especially Shoma. She was being wracked by fierce and violent tremors as if she had extremely high fever. She'd been virtually immersed in icy rain water since her capture.

'Mmmmy … ttteeth … cha…chattering!' she stammered.

'I'll start a fire! Wait here!'

Thanks to her foresight, the huge stack of firewood, pine needles and pine cones were crisp and dry. Brijesh dragged them over to the fireplace and knelt down and arranged the twigs and pine cones. He glanced back anxiously at Shoma. Slumped on the ground, she seemed semi-conscious. He struck a match and the fire took immediately, crackling and popping and fragrant as he fed it and the pine resin lit up, and soon the flames were leaping high and showering sparks. The children crouched as close to the fire as they dared. But in her soaking clothes, heavy with water, Shoma continued to shiver in violent spasms. Hypothermia was not far away; she seemed to be on the verge of losing consciousness; of complete collapse.

'Our cc…clothes,' Shoma stuttered weakly, 'they're ss… soaked.'

'We need to dry them!' Brijesh said hoarsely.

She swayed a bit towards the fire, as his arm shot out and held her back. 'Lllight-headed,' she murmured. 'Dd…dizzy. I th…think I'm going to faint!'

'No!' he barked, 'you can't do that!' And then very gently added, 'now listen, Budgie, you have to take your clothes off right now. You can't stay in those soaking clothes or you'll catch your death of cold.' She just nodded as another tremor violently shook her from head to toe. Her hands went to her blouse buttons but were shaking so much she couldn't place her trembling crinkled fingers on them, let alone undo them.

'Listen,' he said with incredible gentleness, 'I'm going to help you remove your clothes! Is that okay by you? You can change into your old shorts and T-shirt that you've left here.'

She looked at him with wide eyes and nodded. He reached across and gently but swiftly began to completely undress her.

Quickly, he turned his back to her and retrieved the towels and her clothes from the garbage bag.

'Can you rub yourself dry?' he asked. She nodded and took the towel but dropped it. He picked it up.

'Okay, here goes,' he said with a wry grin and began rubbing her down vigorously. She was covered with goosebumps and still shivering uncontrollably. After a while she seemed a little calmer and he wrapped the towel around her snugly.

'Here,' he said, handing her her shorts, 'think you can manage?'

She did, though he had to help her with the T-shirt.

'Don't look now, I have to get out of my clothes too!' he said. He wrapped one of the towels around his midriff. Suddenly he remembered that his mom had once very matter-of-factly told him, on a rainy trek, that the best way for two people to keep warm when they were wet and freezing was to strip naked and hug each other and so share their body heat. He wrapped his arms around Shoma and winced. At the moment, she didn't seem to have any body-heat of her own – her arms and legs were still cold. But he could feel her bird-like heartbeat against his chest and that warmed him wonderfully.

'Better?' he whispered and kissed her gently on the tip of her nose. It was still icy!

'Tha…thanks, you're so sweet,' she murmured, still clutching on to him. Gradually, her trembling ceased. 'Mmm … I'm warm and toasty now,' she said after a while.

'Good,' he said, gently disentangling himself from her and hastily re-tying the towel around his waist, which had begun to come adrift. He picked up her skirt and blouse and then realized that there was something solid in the breast pocket of the blouse. He reached in and pulled out something small and silver that glinted in the firelight. It was almost entirely wrapped up in cling-film, just like his plane.

'What's this?' he asked.

'Oh,' she murmured, 'I ff…forgot – it's Siddharth's recorder. I … I took it to school with me and then wrapped it up in cling-film when it began to rain. I was making rude farty noises into it while riding Grumpy and managed to stuff it in my pocket when they grabbed me and just before they tied my hands. It must still be on unless the battery's died! It must have recorded everything those fellows said on the boat and in the shack and later.'

'Wow! It seems okay,' he said. 'We'll listen to it later – there's just one bar left!' He wrung out her clothes the best he could and then hung them on the stack of wood near the fire, where they steamed gently.

Curled up beside the fire, Big Djinn just watched over them calmly, on guard again.

'Budgie, can you do push-ups?' Brijesh suddenly asked, 'See, like this! They'll keep us warm! They make your heart pump blood around faster, which will warm you!' He dropped down and vigorously began doing push-ups. 'One, two, three, and four ...!' She smiled wanly.

'I'll try,' she said and followed suit.

'Better,' she murmured after a short while, 'I'm much warmer and drier now.'

In the forest outside, the rain thundered down, occasionally accompanied by a shower or two of hail.

'Is there anything to eat?' she asked, pausing after doing several vigorous push-ups. She did feel warmer, much warmer. He thwacked his forehead.

'Yeah, of course, there is, I clean forgot – Kusum Didi made me some jumbo chicken sandwiches. They're in my backpack!'

He fetched the sandwich box and opened it.

Side by side they sat in front of the fire, hungrily devouring their sandwiches, which really were humongous and stuffed to the gills with roast chicken, olives, lettuce, shredded cabbage and carrot, mayonnaise and mustard. Feeling better now—and having shared nearly half their meal with Djinn—they even recovered enough to sneak shy smiles at each other.

'You kissed my nose!' she teased him, pretending to complain.

He went red. 'Uh–huh … it was icy!'

'Hmmm … We'd better stay here until the rain stops,' she went on. 'I hope that … that tidal wave hasn't swallowed up Nani's house!'

'Nah, the house is too high up. But the meadow must have been drowned.'

'Oh crap, and the path around the lake must be under water too. We'll have to find another way back home.'

Then she looked at him, puzzled. 'But how did you turn up at the shack in the first place? Had they captured you too?'

He shook his head and recounted what had happened with the Lancaster.

'And you?' he asked, glancing at her as she leaned over the fire.

'They pounced on me on the ridge top while I was returning from school! One of them caught hold of Grumpy's bridle and the other just yanked me off him. I kicked the fellow in the face really hard, but couldn't do much else. They dragged me down the path and tied me up and stuffed me into that horrible sack and brought me to the shack … The stupid sack was half immersed in water most of the time; I was completely soaked and freezing and nearly drowned.'

'You must have been terrified!'

'Ya, and I was wondering what they'd done to you. You'd said you would pick me up and weren't there … I thought they had killed you!'

She reached out for his hand. 'I … I really like you very much, Bridge,' she said solemnly, 'and thanks for coming after me!'

'And I like you too, Budgie!' he said softly, 'Very, very much!'

They both reached out and petted Djinn and smiled shyly at each other.

'What a dog,' Brijesh said, 'he was just awesome, wasn't he?'

'So, what's the plan now?' Shoma asked. It was getting on to 7.30 p.m. now.

'We'll have to stay here tonight. It's already dark and we don't have any torches. We'll go back tomorrow morning.'

'The rain seems to be stopping,' she said. 'It must have been a cloudburst!'

'Yeah, but I don't trust it. The moment we step out it'll begin again!'

For a while it didn't and all the frogs in the surrounding pools and streams suddenly began singing of love to their lady frogs. Their chorus was accompanied by the steady plink-plonk of water drops falling from the foliage.

'Did you see that?' Shoma asked suddenly, 'Those tiny greenish lights at the corner?'

'Where?'

She pointed. 'Wow!' he breathed, 'they're beautiful!'

'They're fireflies,' she said. 'Look, look, they're coming right in!' For a few astonishing moments, a whole galaxy of fireflies wafted straight into the cave, bedazzling them. They danced around a bit and then flew out back into the dark forest.

'Wow! That was just awesome!'

Suddenly he chuckled. 'Some of them have got caught in your hair – you look like you're wearing winking emeralds!'

She blushed and drew her hand through her tangled curls.

'Let them be, they look lovely!' he protested. She smiled prettily and took his hand.

'Sometimes you say the most idiotic things, Bridge,' she said softly.

They sat beside each other in companionable silence, with Djinn between them – still, alas, reeking of wet dog, but drying off rapidly.

'Hey, maybe we should listen to the recording after all,' Brijesh said, taking out the recorder and switching it on. Eyes widening, they listened: the recording was muffled and tinny and a little indistinct but clear enough. There was enough evidence to jail Shri Suraj Mukhi and his men for life on charges of kidnapping and intent to murder.

'You are amazing, this is gold!' Brijesh said, awed. 'Really, that Suraj Mukhi fellow must be mad! I hope he's drowned, good and proper. He deserves it! He wrecked the whole mountain!' She nodded.

They spread another layer of pine needles on the ground and lay down. It was still very chilly, the cold creeping up from the rocky earth itself into their bones. They snuggled up close, their arms around one another.

'Goodnight, Bridge,' Shoma whispered, kissing him gently.

'Goodnight, Budgie!'

Big Djinn whined again and then, in most un-Djinn-like fashion, wriggled between them. He had sat by the fire throughout and was now at last warm and dry. The children put their arms around him and snuggled up. He was the best warm body they could have asked for.

9

Brijesh stirred at about 2.30 in the morning. For a moment, he wondered where the hell he was, before the events of the previous evening washed over him. Shoma's head was snuggled under his chin, one arm flung around his shoulder, her body draped over his chest. Djinn was now curled up at their feet. He opened one eye and thumped his tail. The fire had died down, though embers flickered and small flames still licked at the remnants of the big branch. But it was getting cold again. Very gently, Brijesh got up and padded to the back of the cave and rummaged for more firewood in the garbage sack. He found a suitable branch and some spindly twigs. He pulled them out and fed them to the fire, blowing hard to encourage the flames to take. Djinn watched him, rumbling approval. The rain had mercifully stopped and the night seemed clear and very cold indeed. Outside, the forest whispered and rustled mysteriously and the night crickets and cicadas and frogs took up their shrill love songs at regular intervals. He sat down beside Shoma, his chin on his knees, and thought about his mother again, the tears beginning to prick and trickle. In a few weeks, he would be back on his way to Mumbai, to stay with that monster that was his father. How would he manage? Lost in thought, he didn't realize that Shoma had awoken, her dark eyes fixed on his face. Wraithlike, she sat up and put her arms around him, and began kissing away his tears.

His arms went around her and he hugged her back tightly and swallowed. 'Budgie,' he whispered hoarsely, 'you know in a bit I'll have to go back to Mumbai. I just don't know how I'll manage with my father.'

'You know, you could always run away and come here and live in this cave,' she said impishly. 'I could bring you supplies and Djinn could keep you company when I'm at school and I could teach you what I've learnt that day so you won't be illiterate …'

He grinned wanly. 'Budgie, you are such a nut!' he said fondly, 'You have no idea!'

'I guess,' she agreed. 'I really wonder what Vinita Aunty and Meatloaf will say when we turn up at home; and those other freaks. Poor Kusum Didi and Annie must be worried sick! They probably think we got washed away in that tidal wave. I just hope they haven't told Nani anything!'

'We'd better get back home as soon as possible, in the morning.'

They lay down and drifted back to sleep. Djinn sighed and closed his eyes, but his ears were still pricked. He was still on guard.

They awoke early the next morning, stirring stiffly and sitting up, for a few confusing moments wondering where they were. Outside, bars of mellow, pale golden sunlight slanted through the trees and the dawn chorus was in full voice. The pines and deodars, so tall, dark and handsome, glittered with raindrops, and gossamer spiders' webs were strung between massive ferns like priceless pearl and diamond necklaces. The earth and soil was moist and rich and fragrant as a fruitcake.

'Wow!' Shoma exclaimed, rubbing her eyes, 'Who would have thought it poured the way it did last evening!'

'Bet it'll be raining again by this evening!' Brijesh said, grinning. 'But yeah, at the moment, it's great!'

Tousled and dishevelled, she smiled at him as Djinn stretched and yawned.

'Come on, we'd better get a move on,' Brijesh said, 'they must be worried as hell back in the house.'

'Nah! Bet that Vinita Aunty and Meatloaf must be thinking that we've been making out like wild things somewhere – and those other freaks must be all agog!'

'Whatever, we'd better get back!'

They slung on their backpacks and set off, Brijesh holding on to his precious Lancaster, still in its cling-film wrap, in one hand. 'I left *Rubadubdub* near where the waterfall goes into the lake,' he said, 'let's check her out. Maybe we could just sail home in her if she's not been wrecked by that wave!'

'That was some tsunami, wasn't it?' Shoma said, taking his hand and threading her way down carefully. 'Careful, these rocks are very slippery!'

They found *Rubadubdub* all right – but the little boat had been hurled inland by the massive wave and now lay upside down a good 50 metres from the shore amidst a welter of broken branches and twigs. She seemed stuck fast between the trunks of two closely growing pines and try as they might, it was impossible to budge her. Besides, there was a huge hole ripped in her hull.

'She's stranded good and proper,' Brijesh panted. 'We can't move her!'

'Better start hiking, it's a long way around,' Shoma agreed.

They would have to trek all along the shoreline of Mehegtal – heading east first, then south and finally west again towards Cloud-house, a good seven or eight kilometres.

'The lake level's risen like anything,' Shoma commented, 'and I've never seen it look so muddy and brown before! It used to be so clear!'

'Well, it swallowed a whole golf course for dinner last night,' Brijesh grinned, 'and must be suffering from a bit of indigestion! But yeah, that lovely flower meadow must be under water!'

'Let's just check out the shoreline,' Shoma suggested. They carefully made their way down towards the banks of the lake. The waters now lapped muddily a good five metres inland and the signs of the devastation wrought by the wave were plain to see. Large boulders lay strewn all over the banks and the wave had flattened the reeds and foliage growing along the banks, even snapping the trunks of young (and very old) pines so that they had keeled over as if knocked over by the shockwave of a bomb. It seemed to be much the same all along the shoreline.

'Will you look at that?' Brijesh whistled. 'No wonder poor *Rubadubdub* didn't have a chance!'

'Come on, let's go back up,' Shoma urged him, taking his hand. 'I don't like seeing Mehegtal in this condition.'

They made their way to higher ground and began walking, keeping an eye on the shoreline through the trees.

'Pity we finished all the sandwiches last night,' Shoma said, 'I'm hungry!'

Djinn had been trotting ahead, his tail swishing jauntily. Suddenly he began to growl. He stopped, looked intently down towards the lake, the growls rumbling steadily and malevolently deep in his throat.

'What is it, boy?' Shoma held him by the collar as Brijesh joined her. Both of them stared down, wondering what had alerted the dog.

'Budgie, look, there's something orange lying there, near those boulders,' Brijesh suddenly said, pointing. Djinn had begun making his way down to the object, his hair standing on end, his growls turning into snarls. The children ran after him.

'Oh my God!' Shoma exclaimed her hands at her mouth, her eyes wide. 'Bridge, do … do you think he's dead?'

'We'd better find out,' Brijesh said.

Their arch-enemy, Shri Suraj Mukhiji, lay flat on his back in the mud, his arms flung out, one leg pinned under the trunk of a young pine tree that had been knocked over by the wave. He seemed to be unconscious – or dead. The children made their way down cautiously, as though approaching a scorpion or cobra, Djinn growling away, his lips drawn back over his teeth.

'Easy, boy!' Shoma told him soothingly, 'He can't harm us now!'

Brijesh was kneeling beside the supine man. He'd been bruised and battered pretty badly, his once immaculate outfit ripped and torn. Then he emitted a hollow groan and Brijesh leapt back, startled.

'Shit – he's alive!' he said hoarsely as Djinn let out an angry bark. Shri Suraj Mukhi, one of the richest tycoons in the country, close friend of the Prime Minister, opened his bloodshot eyes; they flickered from left to right and came to rest first on Brijesh and then on Shoma.

'Beta, bachche, please, some water!' he whispered hoarsely.

Brijesh and Shoma exchanged startled glances.

'Should we?' Brijesh asked, removing a water bottle from his backpack pouch. Shoma nodded.

'I guess,' she said reluctantly. 'He's pretty much pinned down and can't move ...'

Shri Suraj Mukhi tried to raise himself. 'Hari-om!' he cried, as he fell back with a shout of pain.

'Bachche, my leg, I think it's broken! Please help me!'

'Why?' Shoma asked angrily, 'You tried to kill us! You wanted to feed me to that leopard!'

'Nahin bachche, kabhi nahin!' the tycoon replied, lying through his teeth even now, his eyes shifty as always. 'Can you remove this tree from my leg?'

'You did too, you liar!'

'Bachche, can you remove that log? I'm in a lot of pain.'

'Serves you right!' Shoma said hotly.

'Sorry, it's too heavy for us to lift,' Brijesh said – which was pretty much true. But he slopped some water into the tycoon's mouth.

'Bridge, be careful. I don't trust him!'

'Where ... where is this place?'

'You caused the whole mountain, with your precious golf course, to collapse into Mehegtal Lake: what Nani said would happen!'

Specifically, what had happened to Shri Suraj Mukhi was that he had had the luck of the devil. As the pickup had tilted over the edge of the collapsing cliff, its door had swung open and he had fallen out, straight into Mehegtal Lake. By some miracle, he had not been buried under the millions of tons of golf course that cascaded into the lake after him, and managed to cling on to some floating furniture from his villa and was carried clear across the lake on the wave and unceremoniously dumped, unconscious, to where he was now stranded. As if in instant retribution, the tree had come crashing down on his legs right after, pinning him down.

Shoma stood back with her hands on her hips, her eyes flashing.

'You know, mister, you may have all the money and gold in the world but a fat lot of good they're going to do you now! Now your life depends on us!'

'Bachche, what do you want? I'll give you anything you want ...'

'We want that you set right the mountain!' Shoma went on angrily. 'And you can't do that, can you?'

'Bachche, please ...'

Brijesh took Shoma's hand. 'Budgie, let's move on.' He looked contemptuously at the pinned down billionaire. 'We're going now,' he said. He put down his water bottle next to the man. 'We're leaving the bottle here – you can drink when you want to.'

'And maybe, just maybe we'll get help too,' Shoma said, adding viciously, 'Though I hope the leopard or a bear gets to you first! That would be so nice!'

'Please bachche, I'm in a lot of pain ...' He closed his eyes and groaned theatrically.

'Serves you right! I hope they have to cut off your legs with a rusty knife!'

'Budgie!' Brijesh exclaimed, grinning.

They set off again, threading their way through the trees, with Djinn leading the way.

'He'll guide us home,' Shoma said happily, 'he knows all the ways through the forest.'

The rain had triggered off innumerable streams and mini-waterfalls, which were now furiously rushing down the slopes towards the lake.

'We're going to get soaked again!' Shoma said as they stopped beside one particularly excited stream dashing down in a welter of foam, trying to figure a way across. She had put on her school skirt again and now rucked it up. Brijesh simply took off his jeans and T-shirt and stuffed them in his backpack. Very cautiously and holding each other's hands tightly, they crossed as the rushing water blossomed up all around and over them, making them gasp. Djinn leapt light-footedly from one boulder to another and barked encouragement.

'Damn!' Shoma exclaimed, 'I'm totally drenched again!'

They reached the drowned meadow of flowers (now under three feet of muddy brown water) at around 1.30 p.m., tired, footsore and very hungry. Djinn suddenly stopped, pricked his ears and barked. They could hear voices floating across from the direction of Cloud-house.

'Look!' Brijesh exclaimed, pointing, 'Cops! It looks like a search party – and there's Annie with them too!' He cupped his mouth and yelled:

'Hoi! Over here!'

Kusum, Annie and the other staff of Cloud-house had spent the most harrowing evening and night of their lives. Just as the rain had begun thundering down in earnest the previous evening, Grumpy had clopped his way lugubriously to Cloud-house and brayed dismally. Of course, there was no sign of Shoma.

'*Gir gayii hoagie* – she might have fallen off!' Annie said worriedly. 'Come on, let's check!'

But of course, there was no sign of the little girl. At the car park they were told by Hari Singh, who looked after the donkeys, that Shoma indeed had got off her school van and ridden off on Grumpy towards the house. She had asked him if Brijesh was around and then set off. The two women looked at each other.

'Do you think a leopard's taken her?' Kusum dared to ask. Annie shook her head.

'*Grumpy bilkul theek tha*. Grumpy was fine. He would have been injured too if the leopard had attacked.'

Even so, they both knew how stealthily and cunningly a leopard could attack, though it was doubtful that Grumpy would have gotten away without a scratch even in such an encounter. Besides, he hadn't been in the least traumatized or scared, just doleful as usual.

'Maybe, maybe baby's meeting that chokra secretly somewhere. She might have dismounted and gone off with him ...' Annie suggested, raising an eyebrow.

'Could be,' Kusum agreed, smiling now. 'Grumpy might have just gotten bored and come back to the house ... They'll probably turn up on foot when the rain stops.'

'I hope they are able to find shelter.'

Just then, an SUV splashed up the road and the birding team disembarked, sheltering under umbrellas. This time they were accompanied by their two VIP guests, Sir Harold Radcliffe and Dr. Premlata Pushkarna.

'Kusum, some hot sweet tea, please!' Vinita Aunty demanded as soon as they had reached Cloud-house. 'What weather!'

'Where's Brijesh?' Aditi asked Kusum, looking around. 'He's not up in his room ...'

No one had bothered to ask about Shoma, as yet.

'Pata nahin, baby, he went off somewhere in Shoma baby's boat this afternoon, with his plane. And Shoma baby hasn't come back either, though she got off her school van at the car park.'

Aditi's eyes turned into grapefruit as she scuttled off to tell her mother the news and voice her suspicions.

'Ma, it looks like Shoma and Brijesh are secretly trysting somewhere!' she said with a certain amount of relish. 'They must have got caught in the rain ...'

Vinita Aunty looked exasperated.

'That girl is really the limit,' she said, her lips set. 'Just let her get back.' She smiled gratuitously at her guests and offered them more tea.

'Really, my niece who lives here – she's a completely wild child!'

The gang of four huddled together, maliciously conjecturing what Shoma and Brijesh might be doing together in the rain.

But as it became dark, Kusum and Annie began worrying seriously again. It was unlike Shoma to stay out after dark, even if she did have Djinn with her. Something bad might have happened to her or the boy – or to both of them.

And then they heard the deep angry rumble and roar as right across the lake, the pristine new golf course belonging to Shri Suraj Mukhiji came crashing down into the lake and the huge tidal wave swept across in a welter of brown and white, swishing and swilling all over the beautiful flower meadow and actually splashing and then lapping hungrily at the bottom steps that led up to Cloud-house. The birding group watched, white-faced with horror and fear.

'Good God!' Sir Radcliffe exclaimed, 'the whole bloody mountain's collapsed!'

'Some rich fool built a golf course on top of it, so I hear,' Dr. Premlata commented, acidly. 'Must have destabilized the mountain completely, and then with all this rain we've been having ... Well, what do you expect?'

'Madam, we'll have to call the police,' Annie told Vinita Aunty at about 8 p.m., worried sick by now. 'They'll have to search for the children!'

'Annie, no policeman is going to set out in this kind of weather!' Vinita Aunty said as Meatloaf nodded in agreement.

'They must have found shelter somewhere. They'll turn up like bad pennies tomorrow!' Sohan Uncle said. 'Then we can take them to task!'

But neither Annie nor Kusum had slept a wink that night. What if something terrible had happened to the children? They might have got caught in the storm and cloudburst and could have been felled by deadfall. Trees were falling everywhere and rocks the size of houses were tumbling down the mountain sides. The whole mountain had fallen, after all …

Very early the next morning, Annie had set off for the nearest police thana to report the missing children. The cops at the station, including the Station House Officer (SHO), all knew Nani well and were rather fond of Shoma. They had secretly admired the way she had trained that ferocious dog of hers that went with her everywhere. But they were already in bit of a tizzy that morning – news had also arrived that Shri Suraj Mukhiji's brand new resort and golf course and villa had avalanched into the lake. There could be casualties. It was believed that Shri Mukhiji had been there himself too. Search and rescue had to be organized. The SHO telephoned Nainital and even the Army for backup. But he heard Annie out and deputed three trusted men, led by Sub-inspector Balwinder Singh, to go with her and search for the children.

At the resort, the birding group had as always risen early, demanded tea and then set out with their binoculars and cameras. It was too glorious a morning to miss out on.

'Come on, Sir Radcliffe,' Siddharth said excitedly, 'we'll go to the spot where we heard the mysterious birdsong.' He frowned, 'Though I wonder if it will still be around after what happened last evening!' They had to keep to higher ground, of course, and the little tinkling stream was now a raging torrent. But there was no sign of the mystery bird. Disappointed, they returned, had breakfast and then set out for the seminar venue.

'Those children still haven't returned,' Vinita Aunty fumed. 'Really, they are impossible and so irresponsible!' Not for a moment did she consider that some misfortune could have befallen the kids, especially after the kind of rainstorm they had experienced last evening.

The cops had, with Annie, thoroughly beaten around the foliage all along the route from the car park to Cloud-house, thinking perhaps the little girl might have fallen into a khud or ditch.

'*Baba plane le kay gaya* – the baba took his plane. He said he'd be taking Shoma baby's boat …'

'We'll search along the shoreline,' Sub-Inspector Balwinder Singh said. '*Paani bahut upar aa gaya hain*, the water's come very high!' They had raked the muddy lake with their binoculars and seen nothing, of course.

And then at last, they heard Brijesh's excited yell!

'Baby! Baby! Are you both all right?' Annie asked, breaking down as she ran up to the children and took Shoma into her arms in a bear hug. 'You both are very naughty children, running away like this! We've been worried sick! Where did you spend the night?'

'Annie, we're both very hungry!' Shoma replied, hugging her back. 'We'll tell you everything, but let's eat first!'

And so, the prodigals returned to Cloud-house as Kusum disappeared into the kitchen to make them enormous mushroom and chicken omelettes and French toast.

'Where are Vinita Aunty and the others?' Shoma asked, looking around.

Annie screwed up her pert nose. 'They've gone for their precious seminar,' she snorted. 'They think birds are more important than you children!'

Shoma's eyebrows shot up. 'See, I told you Bridge, they don't give a rat's ass about us!'

The cops, now helping themselves to French toast and slurping hot rich tea (made with condensed milk, no less!), radioed back to their thana that the children had been found and were safe and well. But their eyes nearly fell out of their sockets and their ears stood out almost perpendicularly as the children recounted their story.

'*Mukhiji ne aapko jaan se maarne ki koshis kiya – bagh ke saath*? Did Mukhiji want the leopard to kill you?' Balwinder Singh exclaimed incredulously. '*Nahin ho sakta baby*. That couldn't have happened.'

'It did!' the kids chorused, 'And we have proof! Besides, the fellow is lying pinned under a tree some way down the shoreline, so you better go and rescue him. You'll need a stretcher because he's broken a leg.' Shoma took out the silver MP3 player from her pocket. 'Listen to this!'

They were looking very grim indeed at the end of the recording. The matter was now way above Sub-Inspector Balwinder Singh's head and he radioed the thana for instructions. Brijesh quietly took the recorder and nodded. 'I'll make a copy of the recording and then give it to you,' he said, setting up his laptop and sticking a memory stick into it.

'Annie, Kusum Didi – does Nani know that we were AWOL?' Shoma asked. Annie shook her head. 'If you hadn't been found today, we would have had to tell her.'

'Good. Poor Nani would have been so worried!'

'Theek hain sahib!' Sub-Inspector Balwinder Singh said, 'Over and out!' He signed off and looked at the children. 'Can you take us to the place where Shri Mukhiji is?' he requested. '*Hum gaddhe lay jayenge* – we'll take the donkeys. Sahib is sending a medic from the Mehegtal Government Hospital to accompany us. We'll go as soon as he gets here.'

The children exchanged glances and then shrugged. 'Sure, we'll take you to that snake!' Shoma said. They knew it would take a while for the medic to arrive at Cloud-house so they bathed and changed and felt much the better for it. The medic turned up at around 3.30 p.m. Hari Singh had put the whole drove of donkeys at their disposal.

Astride Grumpy and Dumpy, Shoma and Brijesh jogged along comfortably as the cops and medic officer, an earnest young man in a white coat, accompanied them on the others. Big Djinn led the way, of course. They reached Shri Mukhiji in an hour and he seemed to be in pretty bad shape, still pinned down under the tree. Swiftly, the medic got to work as the children watched warily and Djinn growled steadily. The medic set the broken leg in splints after giving Shri Mukhiji a painkilling injection. Then they strapped him onto Stumpy, the calmest and most phlegmatic of the donkeys, and set off homewards.

Back at Cloud-house, the birding group had returned after attending the penultimate session of the seminar. Siddharth had shown his slides to great acclaim and then replayed the mysterious birdsong recordings. They caused quite a bit of excited debate and argument amongst the august guests, though in the end no one could agree on the identity of the mystery bird.

'Son, we'll just have to get a visual,' Sir Harold Radcliffe told Siddharth, 'There's no other way we can identify this fellow!'

To Vinita Aunty's immense annoyance, there had been no donkeys waiting to carry them back to Cloud-house from the car park.

'What do you mean, the police have taken the donkeys?' she asked witheringly, suspecting Hari Singh was drunk. But after they trudged up and down the ridge and finally reached Cloud-house, they found it swarming with policemen. When Annie told them what had happened to the children, Vinita Aunty put her hands on her hips and shook her head, clearly not believing a word Annie had said.

'Shri Mukhiji tried to kill the children? Annie, are you all right in the head? The poor man's brand-new golf course and resort and villa have collapsed into the lake – he must be having a nervous breakdown somewhere!'

'Ma'am, he and his men wanted to feed Shoma baby to a leopard to teach Madam a lesson!' Annie said levelly, somehow controlling her temper. 'The police have gone to arrest him and bring him here! Brijesh bhaiyya rescued Shoma baby last evening just in time, right when the avalanche occurred. He saved baby's life!'

'Annie, I'm not in the mood for nonsense. Now tell Kusum to bring us some tea and something to eat!'

'Very well, ma'am!'

At 6.45 p.m., the rescue party clopped up to Cloud-house. The birding group looked on in sheer disbelief as the cops helped a pale and battered looking Shri Mukhiji off Stumpy. Shri Suraj Mukhiji, perhaps the richest and the most powerful man in India and close buddy of the Prime Minister, was in handcuffs.

'Wh...what?' Sohan Uncle stuttered, 'Inspector, why have you put handcuffs on him?'

'He's under arrest, sir. He will be charged with kidnapping and attempt to murder a child.' He looked at the tycoon. 'Chalo, sahib, let's go!' They put the man on a stretcher and four cops staggered off with him as the others followed.

Standing beside each other, hand in hand, Shoma and Brijesh watched their archenemy lurch away towards the car-park, accompanied by the posse of cops. The gang of four looked on in amazement as did the other members of the birding group.

'I'm glad he's gone,' Shoma said feelingly, 'I hope we never see him again as long as we live!'

'He'll be in jail for a long, long time,' Brijesh said.

Together they went and stood at the top of the steps that led down to the flower meadow and looked across Mehegtal Lake.

'Just look at what he's done to the mountain!' Shoma said sadly. Across the muddy waters, the collapsed mountain looked as if some immense giant had gouged a huge section out of it – a raw wound still unstable with rubble and debris. The top was hollowed out and completely bereft of foliage. They could see the search and rescue teams move gingerly around as they looked for survivors or victims in the rubble.

'But look!' Brijesh said, pointing out. 'Now that the mountain's gone, you can see beyond it to the snow-capped range we couldn't otherwise see!'

He was right. Across the far horizon, the great Himalayan range glittered silver and blue and now, as the sun went down, turned to rich shades of orange and gold.

Vinita Aunty approached them, her face set.

'Shoma, why didn't you ring us and tell us where you were? You have no idea how worried we were! That was most irresponsible of you!'

'Aunty, they threw my phone away when they caught me. And Brijesh doesn't have one – his dad smashed his!'

'So what really happened? You two decided to spend the night together out in the forest and the avalanche happened and you came across Shri Mukhiji?'

'Aunty, didn't you listen to the recording I made?' Shoma asked with some asperity. 'Here, listen to it again!'

They brought out the invaluable silver MP3 recorder and switched it on. Siddharth and Aditi's eyes nearly popped.

'Shoma, that's our backup recorder! We've been looking everywhere for it,' Siddharth exclaimed.

'So you stole that from us too!' Aditi said maliciously as Zit-face and Bony Mouse nodded. 'Chocolate and cheese and energy bars were not enough.'

'You had left it lying in the verandah the other evening and I just borrowed it to listen to the lovely birdsongs you had recorded,' Shoma replied, without batting an eyelid. 'By the way, have you tracked down that mystery bird? Do you know what it is?' she asked, grinning widely.

Sir Harold had wandered up to them, his blue eyes twinkling, and with a drink in his hand. 'No, my dear, we haven't been able to pin it down yet,' he said in his rich, fruity voice.

'Uncle, we'll have another go at it tomorrow,' Siddharth said. 'The session starts late tomorrow so we can search for it till at least 11 o'clock!'

Sir Harold and Dr. Pushkarna nodded. 'Sure, kids, we'll do that! Hopefully that avalanche hasn't scared it away!'

Later that evening, just as they had tucked into a lovely dinner of apple chicken with bacon, broccoli, and fresh salad from the garden, Nani called from Mumbai.

'Nani!' Shoma exclaimed, 'You've now gone to Mumbai? But when are you coming back? We're missing you so much! And do we have a story to tell you or what!'

'Budgie – everything's all right, isn't it?' Nani hardly dared to ask.

'Yes, Nani, everything's fine now! But you know that Suraj Mukhi fellow's golf course and resort fell into Mehegtal Lake after it rained very heavily last evening. The meadow of flowers has been drowned and the lake is looking like muddy coffee!'

'Oh, I did hear something of that kind! I was quite worried but couldn't get in touch because the phone lines were all down, until now! Are you all okay?'

'We're fine. When are you coming back, Nani?'

'In a few days, dear! Now give the phone to Vinita Aunty!'

'Aunty, please don't tell her just yet what happened,' Shoma begged. 'She'll just worry like anything!'

Fortunately, Vinita Aunty saw the sense in Shoma's request and mentioned nothing about what had happened. As usual, the after-dinner conversation was all about birds and the seminar and papers that had been presented. The gang of four, for a change, didn't seem too interested – they were all dying to know exactly what had happened with Shoma and Brijesh last night. Had the avalanche scared them? Where had they gone? Did what they claimed to have recorded really happen? Aditi was simply consumed with curiosity but dared not ask Shoma anything.

Early the next morning, the birding group set off again to look for their mystery bird. Aditi had made a half-hearted attempt to check if Brijesh would like to accompany them but his bedroom door was firmly shut, as was Shoma's.

'Fingers crossed!' Siddharth exclaimed fervently as they set out. 'I just hope we're able to nail the fellow this time!'

And alas, they were both in luck and out of it! They followed the stream amidst the ferns and the rocks where they had heard the bird last and sat down to listen.

'There!' Aditi exclaimed suddenly, 'It's back!' Sure enough, the sad and sweet whistling started off again, becoming cheerful and happy as it went on. And yet again, the bird remained elusive, even from such crack birders as Sir Harold Radcliffe and Dr. Pushkarna. Again, the bird began to sing, went silent and then sang again from a slightly different position.

'It's very restless, isn't it?' Vinita Aunty exclaimed, as Sohan Uncle and Professor Damodar let loose with their cameras, once again in the hope of somehow photographing a bird they couldn't even see! But then the bird fell silent again. Clearly it had flown.

'Damn, damn, damn!' Siddharth said, exasperated. 'It's driving me nuts!'

'Looks like he doesn't want to be seen, just heard!' Dr. Pushkarna commented. 'And he's very good at concealing himself!'

'He's probably very well camouflaged,' Sir Harold said, 'like some of these little warblers are! They're masters of camouflage but give themselves away with their song and calls. But this fellow's a real mystery!'

They wandered somewhat disconsolately back to Cloud-house by around 10.30 a.m., hungry for breakfast. Tired out after their adventure, Shoma and Brijesh had apparently risen late and eaten breakfast and, according to Kusum, were now in Brijesh's room.

'*Baby painting frame kar rahi hain aur bhaiyya plane bana raha hain*. Baby is framing her painting and Bhaiyya is making his plane' she told Aditi and the others.

Which indeed was the case. Aditi slunk up to have a peek. Brijesh's room door was half-open and she could hear the murmur of their voices.

'This shouldn't be too difficult to fix,' Brijesh was saying as he carefully examined his Lancaster. 'But really, that bird ripped out a good chunk from the plane's roof and took the gunner's turret with it! Luckily the camera stayed in place!'

'Mmm …' Shoma murmured as she bent over the painting she was placing in a ready-made frame. Her dad had given her a whole set of them, which she had never used until now. For a long moment, there was silence and Aditi was just about to move away when …

From the room, or more likely the verandah, a long sweet whistle emerged, sad and then happy and cheerful. Aditi's eyes were like grapefruit and her ears almost perpendicular. Quietly, she stole away downstairs and then excitedly summoned the others upstairs, including Sir Harold and Dr. Pushkarna, putting her fingers to her lips.

'The mystery bird – it's right there, probably in Brijesh's verandah!' she whispered. 'Bring the camera! Oh my God, I can't believe it!'

It was still singing. As quietly as they could, they crowded into Brijesh's room, Sohan Uncle with his camera at the ready, and Siddharth already recording. Sir Harold and Dr. Pushkarna suddenly stopped in their tracks, broad smiles beginning to break out on their faces. Sir Harold pointed towards Shoma.

'There's your mystery songbird, Siddharth,' he chuckled as Shoma suddenly looked over her shoulder at them and gave Sir Harold a lovely smile. From the verandah, Djinn, snoozing in the sun, rumbled.

'Wh…what?' Siddharth stuttered. 'It's *Shoma*?'

Shoma grinned cheekily at him as Brijesh began giggling.

'Yes, Siddharth, that's your mystery bird,' she told him, 'I call it Shoma's songbird!'

She pursed her lips and whistled again. Then Sir Harold and Dr. Puskharna's eyes fell on the paintings lying on the floor and bed, awaiting their turn to be framed.

'Dear, are these yours?' Sir Harold dared to enquire.

Shoma nodded. 'Ya, they're mine! Of course, I don't know the names of the birds or anything. I've just painted them as I saw them.'

'But these are just brilliant!' Dr. Pushkarna said, examining one of the watercolours Shoma had done of the falcon. 'You've caught the spirit of the bird just perfectly – all blur and speed and sheer power! You are very talented!'

'My dear, would you mind framing these quickly and showing them at the seminar? There's a celebratory dinner tonight and I'd like to hang these in the room. They're just outstanding!'

Shoma shrugged. 'Okay, I don't mind! I told you I find birds beautiful and cheerful and happy, only I don't like putting them into lists and labelling them this and that! That's almost like caging them. So, I don't know what most of these are!'

'That doesn't matter, dear!' Sir Harold said fervently. He frowned. 'And what's that one you're just framing?'

Shoma looked up and blushed shyly. 'Oh, that's not a bird,' she murmured. 'I ... I did that for Bridge – it's a portrait of his mom.'

'What?' Brijesh exclaimed, craning his head for a look.

'Ya, remember that photograph of your mom that you gave me on the island, Bridge? Well, I based the painting on that.'

Brijesh looked at the painting, his eyes beginning to well up. 'Budgie, it's beautiful,' he whispered. 'Thank you!'

'Anytime,' she grinned and impulsively pecked him on his cheek as Aditi's eyes nearly fell out of their sockets.

That was wonderful but just the half of it. Of course, the birding group had to go back to the seminar and let the participants know the identity of the mystery songster. While the gang of four and their parents and Meatloaf and company would have been quite happy not to mention anything, Sir Harold and Dr. Pushkarna insisted that the truth be told.

'You should have guessed it was Shoma instead of causing such a faux pas!' Siddharth unkindly told his sister. After all, she had been the first to hear and record it.

Poor Aditi burst into tears and ran to her mother for consolation. It would take them a long time to live this down. What made it infinitely more embarrassing was that Sir Harold and Dr. Pushkarna insisted that Shoma and Brijesh accompany them to the seminar hall to hang up the paintings so that the participants could meet and congratulate the artist on her work. Not only that, but some of them (who did have a sense of humour) insisted that she get up on the dais and do her rendition of the mystery birdsong that had caused so much puzzlement. The whole hall erupted in cheers and laughter when, very shyly, she obliged and produced a perfect rendition of her birdsong as Brijesh stood beside her grinning proudly!

A hand shot up after her performance, as a grey-haired lady stood up.

'My dear, but why did you think of doing this in the first place?'

Shoma smiled mischievously. 'Aunty, because I like hearing birds sing, so I decided to try singing like one! Also, it was just so much *fun*!'

Siddharth, Aditi and their parents and the others wished the floor would open and swallow them whole. This was embarrassing beyond belief. Perhaps the only consolation was the fact that even such crack birders as Sir Harold and Dr. Pushkarna had been equally mystified. But it was galling beyond belief! Vinita Aunty smiled thinly and looked daggers at Shoma, who smiled sweetly back at her. This indeed was sweet revenge for having been locked up in a room for a whole day!

But Bridge and Budgie's happiness did not seem destined to last. Late that evening, Nani called again from Mumbai.

Brijesh was being summoned back urgently to sort matters out with his father. Nani had made his travel arrangements. Early next morning, he would leave for Kathgodam by car and from there, catch a train to Delhi and thereon the first flight out to Mumbai. It didn't seem likely that he would return to Cloud-house anytime soon.

10

Very early the next morning, Shoma slipped her dressing gown over her pale yellow pajamas and padded silently into the corridor outside. She noted the line of light under Brijesh's room door: good, he was awake! She tapped softly on the door. She heard him walk up to it and open it.

'Hi,' he said, 'come in. I've just finished packing.' He was in his pajamas too, and a sleeveless pullover.

'This is just so awful!' she said.

'I know,' he replied. 'I knew the day would come, but didn't guess so soon!'

'Do ... do you want to run away and hide in our cave right now?' she asked suddenly.

He smiled wanly. 'That'll only get everyone upset again and your Nani will be in trouble. I don't know what papa wants now!'

'I guess,' she said in a small voice. 'You ... you haven't packed your plane as yet.'

'I'm not taking it,' he said, 'I'm leaving it for you as something to remember me by. I stayed up half the night fixing it – it's done and should fly. We'll fly it the next time I come here.'

'When will that be?' she asked, almost in tears. She gulped; suddenly there was a huge lump in her throat.

'I don't know.' Probably never, he thought.

'You know, Bridge, I really like you so much! I've never liked someone so much before!'

'And I like you very much too.'

She smiled sadly. 'You know, you're the only boy I've seen completely naked from head to toe!'

He grinned back. 'And I saw you naked too – and then hugged you!'

They looked at each other solemnly and moved together simultaneously, clinging close for several long minutes before parting, both with frog-sized lumps in their throats.

She rode with him to the car park and watched him get into the cab that was to take him to Kathgodam.

'He's gone, Big Djinn,' she said desolately, holding her beloved dog and biting back her tears. 'We'll probably never see him again!' Djinn gave her a quick lick.

'Budgie, Bridge and Big Djinn. That's what we are and always will be,' she said fiercely, climbing back onto Grumpy.

She was a desolate and lonely little soul for the next week or so. She had her bike retrieved from the slowly receding waters of the lake. It had languished under water along with Nana's bike that Brijesh had used, near *Rubadubdub's* mooring place. Both were sent for renovation and repair. *Rubadubdub* too was retrieved – and could be fixed! Her entire hull was eventually replaced and luckily, her outboard had not suffered any significant damage apart from a few dents. Vinita Aunty and Meatloaf, alas, were not very sympathetic towards Shoma, who really was a sad little thing those days.

'It's just a silly teenage crush she has on the boy. An infantile infatuation!' Vinita Aunty exclaimed, 'It's high time she got over it instead of pining and weeping like a silly lovesick teenager!'

Aditi, alas, gloated over her cousin's unhappiness. The guy had gone and was probably now flirting with all the hip chicks in his hip school in Mumbai. Serves Shoma right!

While Sir Harold and Dr. Pushkarna left the day after the seminar, the Vermas stayed on and continued with their birding trips. The place really was a haven for birds and they had come here for a whole month and still had some time left. The gang of four, especially Aditi, had stopped being mean to Shoma. The moment any one of them made a sarcastic remark, Shoma would simply purse her lips and whistle her birdsong!

'I wonder what bird that is?' she'd ask, 'Any guesses, Aditi?'

Nani had been held up in Mumbai even longer, but was cagey about the reason and sounded tense and worried on the phone. Shoma had talked to Brijesh on the phone just once and had dissolved into tears afterwards, much to Annie and Kusum's concern.

'*Baby dekho naa, sab kuchch theek ho jayega!* Everything will be fine, Baby!' Kusum consoled her as she wept in the sweet woman's lap.

'How?' she asked hollowly, 'He's in Mumbai and I'm here and he's probably never going to come here again! He was my best friend ever – he saved my life!'

Then Nani called to say she would be returning at last, in two days' time. She sounded relieved and happy. She would be getting back to Cloud-house by late evening and asked that all seven donkeys be waiting at the car park to ferry her home.

Shoma, accompanied by Djinn of course, went to the car park to welcome her grandmother. She was excited, though still pining for Brijesh. At last, she saw the white SUV drive up the slope and nose its way carefully into the car park. Dusk had fallen, and the interior of the vehicle was dark. But Shoma frowned. She could just make out Nani's silhouette in the rear seat, but … but, there seemed to be someone with her.

The driver leapt out and opened Nani's door. Nani emerged tiredly and Shoma ran to her, as Djinn wagged his tail frantically and barked.

'Nani, I missed you so much!' Shoma said, dissolving into tears. She drew back.

'But … but, who's that with you?'

Nani just smiled and held her.

From around the car, a familiar figure emerged, grinning sheepishly at her.

'Bridge!' Shoma squealed, freeing herself from Nani. She flung herself on the boy as Big Djinn barked. 'Bridge, you've come back!'

His grin got wider as he hugged her back.

'Yes, I'm back!' He looked at her as Nani smiled at them. 'And I'm never going back to Mumbai. I'll be living here from now on.' He winked, 'And I'll probably take up birding!'

'What? You're going to live here with us? At Cloud-house?' She couldn't believe her ears. 'Nani, is that true or is he pulling my leg? If he is, I'll kill him!'

'Darling, it's true. It's what his mother had very clearly decreed in her will! I had a hell of a time convincing that obstinate magistrate this was the right thing to do for Brijesh and that his father was in no state to look after him and was violent and abusive and dangerous.' She shook her head. 'But the man was one stubborn and chauvinistic fellow and insisted that the boy must live with his father till he was eighteen. Even after Brijesh had sworn before him that he did not want to and would much rather live with us over here.' She smiled. 'Normally, of course, he would have had to live with his father; that's only natural, but nothing here was natural or normal. And then, his papa solved the problem in his own way. The magistrate was hectoring him about how to be a good parent and so on, when suddenly Brijesh's papa completely lost his head and hurled a chair and a lot of abuse at the magistrate and went after him, actually taking him by the throat and shaking him, before he was dragged off! Well, that decided it! Brijesh's father will probably be institutionalized for a long time – he needs professional care.'

'Oh,' Shoma said, clutching on to Brijesh's hand as if afraid he would vanish into the darkness.

'Brijesh will attend the same school as you, Shoma. I've already spoken to your principal about him,' Nani went on as they ambled steadily up the slope towards the ridge top. Shoma just grinned happily and put her arms around Brijesh's waist and her chin on his shoulder as they rode on Grumpy.

The driver and Hari Singh had unloaded Brijesh's belongings from the car and strapped them on to the remaining donkeys.

'Now what's been going on with you all since I've been gone?' Nani asked. Shoma grinned. 'Brijesh hasn't told me anything … he was just too upset over this whole business.'

'You must have read it in the papers, Nani. Shri Suraj Mukhiji has been jailed for trying to kidnap and murder me! He wanted to feed me to a leopard so he could teach you a lesson for not selling him Cloud-house! But Bridge and Big Djinn saved me in the nick of time and we escaped and had to spend a night in a cave and …'

'*What?*' Nani exclaimed. 'And no one told me a thing!'

In Mumbai, poor Nani had hardly had the time to read the newspapers properly or watch the news on television, she'd been so involved with her lawyer in preparing the case for Brijesh.

'Nani, we didn't want to worry you! Besides, that Vinita Aunty and Meatloaf hardly believed our story anyway until the police turned up. They thought we had run away together, can you imagine!'

'Young lady,' Nani barked with some asperity. 'The moment we reach home and settle down, you both will sit down and tell me *everything!*'

'Sure, Nani,' Shoma said demurely. She put her mouth to Brijesh's ear and whispered happily.

'And we'll be Budgie, Bridge and Big Djinn, happily ever after!'

Epilogue

Brijesh settled down in Cloud-house very quickly indeed and very happily, and he and Budgie (and Big Djinn, of course) were virtually inseparable. When Shoma's dad, Dalbir, heard what had happened, he made a flying visit and ordered that *Rubadubdub* be completely overhauled. Within a fortnight, Brijesh had taught Budgie how to swim in the same pool at the base of the waterfall. The children made their cave even cozier by furnishing it with more cushions and rugs, blankets, some mugs and cutlery – and stacks of firewood, of course. Every weekend, the three of them first went fishing in Mehegtal Lake (which had slowly regained its pristine purity) and then cooked up their catch in their cave or up on the island.

The Lancaster bomber flew again, many times, though the children kept a sharp eye out for the falcon, which seemed to have gotten used to the plane and ignored it.

Of course, the press turned up en masse to cover the story – after all, one of the nation's richest men, a confidant of the Prime Minister, was the main accused in a murder conspiracy and had brought down an entire mountainside! But as with the press everywhere, they lost interest quickly and disappeared.

The terribly scarred mountain just across the lake remained an eyesore and grim reminder of what had happened. When villagers in the surrounding areas and residents of Mehegtal heard the story, they convened a meeting one Sunday soon afterwards, and were joined by local NGOs, and students and teachers from the surrounding schools and colleges. It was decided that they would try to afforest the devastated mountainside. Luckily, there were several veteran villagers amongst them who had ideas of how this might be done – and had done it before, albeit on a smaller scale.

It was decided that they would first construct low embankment walls in parallel rows, a few feet apart, right across the mountainside, along the entire length of what had once been the short-lived golf course. Channels would be cut in these, for drainage, so that excess rain water would simply run down into the lake and not cause erosion. The area between the embankments would then be packed with a mixture of gobar and soil stuffed with the seeds of grasses that grew in the area. It was hoped that the dung-beetles and earthworms would do their job and the grasses would take hold in the rich new soil and firm up everything. Birds that came to feed on these seeds would drop other seeds of fruiting flowering trees. Eventually, the villagers would attempt to plant bushes and trees – rhododendron, oak and sal and other broad-leaved varieties.

Of course, it would take years to regenerate the forest and cost a lot of money – though all of this, the courts had declared, would be paid for by the fines imposed on the Shri Suraj Mukhi Development Enterprises. The villagers and local people and students would provide free labour and half the gobar their livestock produced.

A fleet of trucks (called the Gobar Gaadi Fleet!) was requisitioned from Shri Suraj Mukhi Enterprises and went around the area every day, collecting gobar and soil, and chugged up the mountain slope where the labour awaited them. Most weekends and holidays, Shoma and Brijesh would be up there along with children from their and other schools, patting down the dung and soil into place.

Some six months later, you could discern the faintest shimmer of green on the slopes. Grass had taken hold, and with it, wildflowers had begun blooming.

'It looks like we're going to have a new flower meadow!' Shoma said delightedly.

'It's better than bare rock, certainly!' Brijesh agreed. 'Actually, they should bring Shri Suraj Mukhi and all his men here to repair the damage.'

Shri Suraj Mukhiji was still in Nainital jail awaiting trial and would remain there for a long time to come. Once evidence had been provided of what he had done to the pristine mountain, along with the attempt to so cruelly kill a little girl in order to acquire even more property, all hell had broken loose. The justice system had absolutely no sympathy for him. He was eventually found guilty by every court he appealed to, right up to the Supreme Court, and would stay in jail for the rest of his natural life. His companies would have to pay the entire cost for the rehabilitation of the mountain he had destroyed. Several of his men had died when the golf course had collapsed – he had been very lucky indeed to have escaped alive.

The Prime Minister, of course, had vehemently denied that he had ever known the man! 'So many people want to have their photographs taken with me – I hardly know most of them!' he said, when shown footage of himself warmly embracing Shri Mukhiji at some function.

*****

We must fast-forward forty years now …

Nani died shortly after Bridge and Budgie got married (as was inevitable!), around ten years later. Her death reminded Bridge of his own mom's death, so many years ago. But now he smiles wanly and tells Budgie, 'You know, if mom hadn't died it would have been really great, but then I wouldn't have come here and met you and be sitting here with you today!'

And Budgie adds: 'Yes, Nani always used to say that when one door closes, a window somewhere opens!' And then goes on: 'Of course, it would have been wonderful if the door didn't have to close in the first place and the window opened anyway!'

Once, when they were both in a somewhat maudlin, sentimental mood, Budgie asked Bridge with a mischievous smile: 'So when did you first realize that you were falling hook, line and sinker for me?'

'Umm ... on *Rubadubdub* that first morning you took me out, when you said I was as good as, if not better than God!' And added: 'Of course I am! And you?'

'Well, it was kind of gradual: a bit when I realized that Big Djinn approved of you, a bit on the boat, when you helped me with the fish but didn't snatch the rod away and reel the fellow in all on your own – but mostly, in the cave when I had nearly frozen to death and you asked me if I minded if you undressed me because I couldn't manage to do that myself. That really got me!'

Brijesh became a brilliant aircraft designer and engineer and spent many years in the USA, independently designing planes and engines and computer systems for various aircraft manufacturers. Then, one fine day, he gave it all up, sold his company and he and Shoma returned to Cloud-house, where he still designs, builds and flies his own remote-control models (but not drones, which he doesn't like at all!).

Shoma became a well-known artist and painter, and has held shows and exhibitions around the world. Her work sells for really incredible sums.

She and her once arch-enemy cousin Aditi have made peace and laugh (somewhat sheepishly) while recalling their terrible catfights. Shoma accepts that in order to protect birds, you need to identify and study them scientifically and make lists and classify them properly. Aditi has also appreciated that some people (like Shoma) are drawn to birds and nature in a more subjective and emotional way, which is equally valid and valuable.

Budgie and Bridge have two lovely daughters – the elder, Sameera, now a practicing vet (and wild animal rescuer) in Mehegtal, and the younger one, Shreya, doing her PhD in Botany, specializing in medicinal plants.

The third generation of the Djinns now guards Cloud-house and its inhabitants. The two huge dogs patrolling the property have been called Lord Djinn and Lady Djinn, and both protect Sameera and Shreya as fiercely as Big Djinn had done Shoma.

Kusum's niece now runs the Cloud-house Home-stay (still as exclusive as it had ever been) and is married to Annie's son, who is the major domo in charge of the property's maintenance and stable of 12 donkeys and 5 hill ponies.

The Lancaster bomber rests in a glass case in the big drawing room, and the portrait that Shoma had painted of Brijesh's mom hangs in their bedroom.

Best of all, though, is that the shattered, barren mountainside across the lake is now covered with oak, sal and rhododendron forests and is guarded fiercely by the locals.

But as Shoma tells Brijesh as they sit on the verandah looking across the lake, 'It took that monster just two or three years to lay waste and bring down an entire mountainside – and it's taken us 40 years to bring it back to life.'

ABOUT THE AUTHOR

Ranjit Lal is the author of around 45 books – fiction and non-fiction – for children and adults who are children. His abiding interest in natural history, birds, animals and insects is reflected in many of his books: *The Crow Chronicles, The Life and Times of*  *Altu Faltu, The Small Tigers of Shergarh; The Simians of South Block and the Yum-yum Piglets, The Tigers of Taboo Valley, Bambi, Chops and Wag; Birds from My Window; The Birds of Delhi; Wild City, The Trees of Medley Gardens, The Little Ninja Sparrows, Rumble in the Jungle* etc.

His book, *Faces in the Water*, on female infanticide, and for which he was honored by IBBY in 2012, won the Crossword Award for Children's Writing 2010 and the Laadli National Media Award for Gender Sensitivity 2012.

Our Nana Was a Nutcase – on dementia and Alzheimer's – won the Crossword Raymond Award for Children's Writing in 2016.

Other books with social themes include *Taklu and Shroom* (shortlisted for the Crossword Award for Children's Writing 2013), *Miracles, Smitten* (on child abuse in the family), *The Secret of Falcon Heights, The Dugong and the Barracudas, Bozo and Chick, The Battle for No. 19, The Hidden Palace Adventure, Bozo and Chick* and *Owlet, Not Out.*

He was awarded the Zeiss Wildlife Lifetime Conservation Award for 2019 for writing 'with exceptional literally skills' on the conservation of wildlife, especially birds.

As a journalist, he has had well over 2000 articles and photo-features published in the national and international press and currently has a column – *Down in Jungleland* – in the Indian Express 'Eye'. He also writes a monthly children's column for the Hindustan Times called *Bratpack Brief.*

His other interests include photography, automobiles, reading and cooking. He lives in Delhi.